THE

LIES

WE

BURY

JOE COBB CRAWFORD

This book is a work of fiction. References to real
people, events, establishments, organizations,
or locales are intended only to provide a sense of
authenticity, and are used ficticiously. All other
characters, and incidents and dialogue, are drawn
from the author's imagination and are not to be
construed as real.

The Lies We Bury
Copyright @ 2015 The Poetry Company, LLC.
All rights reserved.

Developmental Editing by John A. Shivers
Copy Editing by Scotty Plappert
Cover Design by LifeSprings, LLC
Type and Layout by Dianne VanderHorst

Published by Laurel Mountain Press
P.O. Box 1973 Clayton, Georgia 30525
laurelmountainpress@windstream.net.

Printed in the United States of America
ISBN: 978-0-9888374-5-4

To the brave men and women who choose each day
"to Serve and Protect"
we the people

Table of Contents

THE
DEATH

PART I- Section 1

2006- Fall of the Year

"And what do all the great words come to in the end,

but that? I love you- I am at rest with you -

I have come home."

From *Busman's Honeymoon*, by Dorothy L. Sayers

Chapter 1 - CREEKSIDE

Loud mountain creekside
Silent shot, lone wistful prey
Slain heart streamed away

The old van with the cracked windshield was parked at Curtis Switch Crossing. From there he launched his craft into Fighting Town Creek's green water. In the somber pre-dawn hours, he floated solo between silhouetted hills and ridges. Morning moonbeams highlighted the inflated raft's course. To the left and right, emerald laurels defined its narrow boundaries. In the middle, farther downstream, the needles of light fluoresced from the whitecaps.

Where the lapping waters of Mill Creek merged, eddied, and frothed, he stopped. There he tied up to an overhanging spruce. Boots on the ground and his assault weapon shouldered, he marched up Mill Creek, through the green marshes with pointy rushes and lush knife-edged leaves. Just short of Lee Cornwell's cabin site, he made his way. A distant dog barked once. The soldier froze in place. Fifteen minutes he stood motionless, sensing. Twenty minutes shy of daylight he entered the woods, following a rocky deer trail leading up a knoll overlooking the meadow.

He held his weapon at his side. Dropping to one knee he lifted the crime scene tape and dipped under it. He marched to a location in the undergrowth with a clear view of the meadow. The soldier sat, rested, reflected on his mission until sunrise. The dog barked again, just once. *Enemy territory infiltrated. Phase one complete,* he told himself.

———————

My dreams aren't ended, only delayed for a few days, Lee Ellen Cornwell assured herself. Her law enforcement career had taught her that the wheels of justice do in fact turn slowly. Unlike most, she knew this from twenty-three years in the trenches. Her experience provided more than a placating philosophy.

She also knew the crime scene tape surrounding her mountain cabin site carried authority—as much as a battalion of heavily armed blue suits. She dared not challenge its authority. She would wait until all legal matters had cleared before setting foot on her cabin's building site.

Still, there were things she could do before the building started. Anything beat whiling away hours reading, holed up in her camper at Morganton Point, Georgia. *I'll drive down to Mill Creek. I won't cross the line. At creekside I can stand and observe and envision*

how my cabin will look situated up there on the knoll.
May see something I've missed.

This she did each morning after the crime scene tape was installed. Her Bronco she parked beyond the bend in the Old Epworth Road, behind a pine thicket, just out of sight. Every day an old lop-eared hound dog greeted and hung out with her on the daily trek. They traveled along the creekside. With reckless abandon the trotting dog raced, sniffed the ground, marked the bushes, and stepped on her feet—occasionally tripping her.

They continued their awkward haphazard pace. She'd stop and leisurely listen to the random noise of the rushing water, watching for darting minnows and flitting snake-feeders. She listened to cawing crows sailing a blue sky or roosting in a tall pine overlooking the lush meadow.

Destination achieved, half-smiling she stopped, faced the knoll, and placed her hands on her hips. The blinding tunnel light drowned out everything.

The soldier watched her collapse and tumble into the creek. He lowered his cross bow, inhaled deeply and gave an affirming nod. He told himself: *Perfect—straight through the heart—I still got it.* He cut his eyes left then right, turned facing down the creek, and plotted his retreat. In reverse order, he retraced his path back to his waiting raft.

The old dog was confused. He mistakingly thought she was being playful. Following suit, he too, jumped into the creek, splashed about, and let out a yelp. Seeing no reaction, he froze in place. Tail held high, he crept to the lifeless body. He sniffed the broad-head arrow's stem and point. With head bowed and neck stiffened, like a rooting wild hog he nudged the body.

Blood flow was minimal. The heart had stopped pumping instantly. A trickle slowly comingled and clouded a small edge-water puddle. Quickly it was sucked into the fast-moving creek.

The soldier's past Army training and more recent survivalist exercises had served him well. His controlled pace delivered him back to the raft before the sun stood over the meadow. Carefully he covered the spare arrow tips and placed them and the crossbow into the raft's bottom. Rope untied, he lunged in, collected a paddle, and maneuvered to mid-stream.

As the Blue Ridge tourist train's whistle announced its McCaysville arrival, he pulled ashore.

The water was deep, calm, and somber. With red bricks he'd carried in the raft and nylon cords, he tied and sank the crossbow and the quivers at the bottom of Fighting Town Creek.

He set sail again, and floated until he reached the Ocoee River. A motor scooter was chained and waiting there for him. In the Ocoee, he shoved out the raft, watched it gain speed and drift toward the Tennessee line.

Twenty minutes later, he was back to Curtis Switch. He loaded the motor scooter into the van. Gazing through the cracked windshield, he confidently told himself, *HOOAH!*

———

Chapter 2 - LIFE AND OTHER ILLUSIONS

Lee Ellen's funeral was emblematic of her life—brief, low keyed, full of contradictions and ironies. Most ironic about the ceremony, was the attendees. Her two living siblings were there as expected, but fellow law enforcement officers from Atlanta were few, while mere acquaintances were disproportionately well represented. People whose name she would not have remembered packed the church's pews. A member of the Fannin Sheriff's department and the local newspaper were there. People from her hometown, those whom she had not seen in years attended. They sat at the back and held court on other attendees.

Two, past fifty ladies whispered incessantly. They were overheard to say:

"Look there Gladys, up there on the second pew. That man on the right. Know who that is?"

"Well, no. I don't know him from Adam's house cat, but he's good-looking. Got broad shoulders. Nice hair. Who is he?"

"That's her ex, Mark Cornwell. He's the one she sent to prison. Smoking dope, drinking, carrying on, him and his drug buddies was when he's supposed to been watching their baby boy."

"You don't say.   Cleans up good for a convict. How long was he in for?"

"Not long enough, if you ask me.   Little boy got out of the apartment.   Got hit by a car, but he lived."

The church got quiet.   Footsteps echoed.   Six single-file pallbearers, led by the funeral director marched to the church's front where the casket lay covered with flowers.   All pallbearers wore the blue uniform.   They sat on the front pew.

The minister rose from his throne-like chair and motioned for all to stand.   He led them in a prayer and then motioned for them to be seated.   Accompanied by a poorly tuned piano, a portly young lady sang "I Come to the Garden Alone."   The minister followed by reading lengthy sections of various scriptures.   He made a few comments alluding to the funeral being a celebration. Few who truly knew Officer Lee Ellen Cornwell were buying what he was selling.

The ceremony ended abruptly.   Led by the funeral director, the pallbearers rolled and loaded the casket into the waiting hearse.   Lee's friends and other specious attendees rose from their padded pews.   From the small church they shuffled out.   Each appeared saddened, but held their heads high. Their faces looked relieved as they left the church. They had absolved their tinge of guilt. The right thing had been done—the prescribed protocol had been nobly executed. It was all folks could do considering the circumstances; all in keeping with local traditions regarding this matter of accidental death.

Later, another traditional obligation would be met. They would reconvene in the church's adjoining fellowship hall and would eat together. A prayer would be uttered and they'd comfort themselves with deviled eggs, barbeque, and other southern fried favorites.

The church's appearance had changed since she attended there as a child. Located in the tall oaks, the once egg-shell colored clapboard church on Hog Back Road was now armored in red brick facade. No remnant of yesteryears' adjacent muddy parking lot sparsely sprinkled with gravel was visible. A glistening fresh coat of asphalt masked its red clay base. White lines marked each designated parking place—minister, staff, visitor and handicapped. Today, all was elegant and spotless. Tall shrubs, spiral junipers, and cone-shaped hollies softened the building's once edginess and skeletal protrusions. But little had really changed—not the church, the church people, or their ways.

Fifty years had passed since she last attended

there. She had lived most of her life away from her beloved Blue Ridge Mountains. Those were the days before she received the dress—the one she thought would shape her youthful figure. It did not. The dress shaped her future mindset.

———————

THE
GIRL

1961- Spring of the Year

"There is none righteous, no, not one."

From The Holy Bible, Romans 3:10

Chapter 3 - THE CHURCH DRESS

They were the ones who had taken up a love offering to give to her grandmother—the grandmother who took them in, Lee and her four siblings, after their mother abandoned them that Christmas. It was the same church whose one member had given her that store-bought dress.

The dress screamed exuberance with its bountiful floral design, not like those leached barren hills and rain-carved gullies surrounding its place of purchase. Back then the store had been the finest provider of apparel to be found in this remote rural area. It was known for miles around as The Company Store and was located across the Ocoee River in Copperhill, Tennessee, a copper mining town and the twin city of McCaysville, Georgia.

Her dress brimmed with daisies and daffodils and touch-me-nots. Enamored by the dress, she would steal away to admire it. She'd look at it up there, suspended and hanging from a hook in her bedroom's ceiling. She wondered, *How will I look in that dress? Will I be the same person when I wear it? What will people say about me?* Her older sister's hand-me-downs were her usual attire. She dreamed of the day she would wear her beautiful new dress.

On Easter morning her dream came true; Lee wore the dress to church. The church member who had given her the dress met her in the vestibule and told her, "Lee, bless your heart, you look absolutely beautiful. You come and sit with me, honey." Lee left her older brother and sister and two younger siblings seated on the back pew. She was led by the lady to the middle of the church and there was told, "We'll sit right here, honey child. You sit here on my right. I need to sit closest to the aisle." Lee complied without question.

She was indeed a beautiful little girl and the dress fit her fine. Her bright blue eyes, her thick blonde hair, and her pearly fresh smile epitomized spring itself. She sparkled like a diamond seated beside her kindhearted friend that Easter morning. Up front as the congregation slowly filed in, keys struck on the piano sent forth a melody of hope, assurance, and expectations. "He Lives" resonated through the rafters as sun rays channeled through the church's un-draped windows, spilling onto the slat board pews.

Lee Ellen was a perceptive and cautious little girl—always alert, sensitive, and quick on the uptake. Later in life those instincts and intuition would keep her safe in her sworn duty to protect and serve. Today, she observed that each entering congregant was stopped and conversed with by her generous and caring friend. Lee suspected, yet did not want to believe she was partaking in a ruse intended to showcase her trusted friend's Christian charity. Lee noted a pattern: Her friend briefly spoke to each and then diverted their attention to the beautiful dress. Proud as punch each was told, "You know? The Company Store gave me a ten percent 'benevolence discount' on this dress I got for her. Doesn't she look simply precious in that dress?" After the third refrain from her friend's self-praising hymn, Lee had heard enough and took action.

Out of the blue, with tears streaming, she sprang from the pew. She raced down the aisle to the church exit. The friend and her captive audience were "fall-out-of-bed" stunned when Lee made her escape. Question marks traced their twisted-up faces. Descending the church's steps Lee pulled frantically at the frilly lace, tearing it from the Easter dress and throwing it to the ground. More than a drowning person wants air, she wanted the dress not to touch her. Like a scarlet letter it announced to Lee and told her "you are grimy and worthless, nobody loves you, but most of all it told her, 'You don't belong here.' In her mind, it was a badge telling all of her inferior status. All she wanted now from her dream dress was to be absent from it.

Through a back road and a dusty trail lined with saw briars she navigated her way home. She had walked this path before and was familiar with the deer trails and mountain short-cuts. In no time she entered her only refuge, her grandmother's house. The squeaking screen door slammed shut as she ran to her bedroom.

"Lee, what's wrong, honey? Why ain't you at church?" her grandmother demanded, while wiping her hands on her apron, as she marched to Lee Ellen's bedroom. Opening the door she saw the dress. Discarded and out of place, it piled up despairingly there on the bare bedroom floor like a spent gum wrapper. She also observed the blood on Lee Ellen's ankles, the blood caused by saw briars. Without asking more questions her grandmother turned and scurried away. Soon she returned with a wash cloth and Mercurochrome, which she applied to the scratches.

"Baby, did someone hurt you?" she asked while scanning Lee's naked body.

"No, Granny" she muttered, but said nothing more.

Her gaping mouth stayed parted as she sat in the center of her bed. Suppressed whimpers and tears soon morphed into hushed groans. With palms up, her arms lay limp at her sides like two willow branches. She had felt nothing when her grandmother's firm hands removed the blood and treated her scratched ankles. Staring into space Lee found no words to tell her grandmother all she was feeling—about the new dress and about the lady at church and about those in whom she had placed her trust, thinking they loved her.

These were the seminal pangs of the woman who today was shielded by a flag-draped coffin. Those pangs were complicit: From them, a life of harrowing times was born.

———

PART I - Section 2

1966 - Late Fall of Year

"Larceny is not a difficult crime to condone unless
your childhood was the item stolen."

From *The Prince of Tides*, by Pat Conroy

CHAPTER 4 - SHE NEVER WORE
THAT DRESS AGAIN

Ed Bandy carefully set his cigarette on the glass ashtray's edge. On an end table covered by a white doily, it rested there beside the faded Davenport where he sat reading the *Atlanta Constitution*. As the cigarette smoldered, sending a keen stream drifting toward the small room's ceiling, he placed the heel of each hand over an eye. Slowly he massaged each as though buffing bondo from a restored bent fender—a job he had done since he was a teen. The whites now pink, Ed's eyes locked in on Lee Ellen and he began his measured terse words:

"Young lady, you are going with me and don't you give me none of your lip. Momma ain't able to keep up with the shenanigans you and that boyfriend of yours got going on. You'll go and stay with me in Marietta, and that's final."

An angry but assertive Lee Ellen fired back, "Daddy, I don't want to live in Marietta. I don't have any friends in Marietta. This is my home and I'm staying put, right here with Granny." Turning to her grandmother she then said, "Granny, tell him I can stay here with you."

Lee's grandmother sat solemn as Lincoln's Monument in her rocking chair saying nothing. Not because she had no opinion on the matter, but because with age she had become wiser. She knew the circumstances were not simple and the decision was not hers to make.

Silence filled the dimly lit room. All that could be heard was the simmer and sputter of green oak wood burning inside the Warm Morning heater. Ed lifted his cigarette, sucked in a puff, and set it back in the ashtray. Then he stared at the floor. Her dad's quiet treatment was not what Lee had hoped. "Yes" was the decision she wanted. Sensing her words had not been heard, she fired up again: "Daddy, I ain't going down there with you. In the summer, when school is out, Tommy and I are getting married." With a half-smirk on her face, Lee continued, "We done been to Snead's Jewelers in town looking at wedding rings. He gave me his senior class ring to wear until we can afford real rings." An air of confidence now swept Lee's face. She daintily held her hand out, flexed her wrist down so her dad could see it—the make-do ring, a massive, gnarly gob of fake-gold with "West Fannin High School" boldly embossed on its perimeter. The ring fit poorly.

Located below a yellow stone, a cross-wrapped rubber band held the ring on her small finger.

Ed cocked an eyebrow, dusted his cigarette ashes, and asked, "Tommy Duke? Is that who gave you that ring? Yeah, I know his daddy, Sam Duke... dumber than dirt. Old Dumb Duke, is what everybody called him when we was growing up out in Caldwell. I tell ya, that Sam was so dumb that if he threw himself at the ground, he'd miss. And his older brother Jack Duke, he wasn't much smarter. He's so dumb he made yard chickens eating gravel look smart. Lee...you ain't marrying nobody from that dumb Duke family. You are going with me to Marietta. Now I done told you how it has to be."

Granny held her silence. She knew that neither Ed nor Lee was listening to each other. She rose from her rocking chair and struggled to stand erect. Her shaky, liver spotted hand reached for her walking cane. She got a grip on the handle and hobbled toward the kitchen. Not looking back, she muttered, "You two need to hush-up for now. Just table it. Everybody's talking and ain't nobody listening. I'll have dinner done in a bit." Entering the kitchen, she opened the wood stove's oven door and checked on the cornbread she was baking for Sunday dinner.

Lee's eyes had followed Granny's feeble steps as she went out of sight. Seeing Granny leave the room, Lee picked up a yellow West Fannin letter jacket—the jacket Tommy earned playing two years on the football team. She turned and saw her dad fumbling and rattling the paper, looking for the *Sports Section.* Ed never missed reading Furman Bisher's column. Walking toward the front door she glibly told him, "Daddy, I'm going for a walk and to see if there's enough snow to make a snowman." As she opened the front door, a frigid gust of air rushed in. Standing in the doorway, Lee buttoned up Tommy's coat and viewed a winter vista—a rabbit tracker skiff of snow set against snow-capped blue mountain peaks.

Ed tried not to let his daughter see it, but she had caught him off guard. He wasn't prepared to deal with her defiance. At the same time he had been impressed. His daughter was growing up and could clearly hold her ground and speak her mind. He had always known she was more like her mom than any of his other four children—intelligent, intuitive, but strong willed.

Ed was cut from a different cloth, but he knew

and accepted this about himself. A man of few words, conservative in all views of life and one who was more uncomfortable than most when in Sunday church clothes. These were virtues "caught and not taught" by his mountain upbringing. He was a true North Georgian—poor, but proud. Through drive, sweat, and determination, and little else, Ed was a self-made man. He worked hard with his hands to support his five children. He had scabs on his knuckles and grease under his fingernails, and Lee had been moved to tears more than once after seeing her daddy's hands bleed from the rough work he did to make them a living. Until a year ago he had worked for a Blue Ridge auto dealership. Business fell off and they had to let him go. Now he had a better paying job in the big city, in Marietta, Georgia.

His wife, Mary Beth, was a contentious, patronizing woman, never passing up an opportunity to question any decision Ed made. Unlike Ed, she was a city girl and her family had things—things Ed could never get for her. When chatter slowed at the Blue Ridge Beauty Salon, the gossips always trotted out Ed and Mary's marriage to discuss. They wondered aloud how this mismatched two ever got together. Mary never voiced it, but she did think she was smarter than Ed. Irish to the bone, she would fly off the handle when Ed ignored her spoken opinions on decisions he made. He would sometimes stop her midway through her fits and matter-of-factly tell her, "Mary Beth, two mules pull this wagon, and I'm the lead mule and the man of this house." One such out-of-control, bitter quarrel was the last straw for Mary and it sent her packing, never to return to the house, to the mule barn, or to her five children.

Lee was turned a little odd like her mom, but differed from her in at least one way. She was not inclined to run from a fight, be it physical or a war of words. Like her mom, Lee thoroughly enjoyed a good battle of wits, but unlike her, she had been taught by her granny that sometimes you have to lose in order to keep the peace. "Take one for the family" was how Granny put it.

The present quarrel would go on this way. Her unspoken plan was to concede to her Dad's demands, but thinking in the back of her mind, I'll go stay in Marietta a few days and then I'll come back home to stay with Granny—here where I have Tommy, where everybody knows my name, and no one's a stranger. When she returned from her walk she felt less strongly about not wanting to go with her dad.

Lee gathered up her clothes and her sparse belongings and packed them into the back of her dad's stationwagon. While hunting for her things, she opened a cedar chest and saw the church charity dress lying at the bottom of a pile of second hand clothes. The sight re-opened an old wound. She never wore that dress again, after what happened that day over five years ago. Reflecting now on that time made moving away seem not such a bad idea. Besides, Tommy and she had always planned to move to the Atlanta area after they married. There was no place in the mountains to make a living. Lee always had a plan B and was two steps ahead of others' plans for her.

———————

CHAPTER 5 - IT'S ALL ABOUT THE TEAM

S canning the apartment, Lee reckoned it to be about as empty as a bird's nest in December. Her eyes came to rest on a door so narrow that one could skinny through it only by turning sideways. She dropped her army surplus duffle bag on the gaudy gold shag carpet. "Daddy, where is the bathroom?" she asked, turning and searching for anything that resembled a bedroom.

"Honey, it's right there where you're looking— straight ahead through that little door."

Still scoping out the humble abode she continued, "O.K., but where do you sleep in this place? I don't see nary a bed anywhere."

A smile tugged at the corners of Ed's tight lips as he watched Lee. Winking his left eye, he snickered, turned, and said, "Watch this." His hand reached high on the wall where a recessed shiny handle hid. Tugging at the handle with one hand and with the other pointing like an *Uncle Sam Wants You in the Army* sign, he boldly announced, "It's a Murphy Bed." A bed not much larger than an army cot came clanging out and fell to the floor. Stunned by the squeaking and thumping noise as it crashed to the carpet, Lee jumped back. She thought to herself, Oh shit! Daddy's done tore up the wall and broken the onliest bed in this place.

Ed's dentures now beamed wide and bright like the grill on a 1953 Buick. He patted and smoothed the sheet on the little single-mattress bed and took a seat. Then, after plugging a cigarette between his lips and lighting it, he dangled and motioned with his other hand toward a petite couch. One missing leg had been replaced with a cinder block, and its covering was oversized flower petals. He said, "You can sleep here or you can sleep on that couch. Don't make me no never-mind. I can sleep either place."

Mixed feelings of fear and hope shined through Lee's wet eyes. She tried hiding her uneasiness, but wrinkles remained on her brow. Ed knew that look, the one that always told him he had failed. He had seen it before; he knew the look to be real—warm and true like a fresh laid egg, but at the same time more cutting than a kidney stone. This time that look told him he could no longer delay telling her what he had kept secret from the rest of the family for too long.

He said, "Lee honey, sit down a minute. There is something I need to tell you." Pausing a minute, he nervously flexed one hand while taking quick puffs on his cigarette. Then, in an ashtray that sat on the floor he stubbed out his cigarette and disclosed the dreaded truth:

"Ya see honey, I know this place don't look like much, but we're not going to be here long. I'm figgerin' on moving us in just a few days to a bigger place. You'll have your own room there. You see, Lee, I'm fixin' to get married. Her name is Donna Gray and we'll be moving to her house. It's not far from here."

"Married?! Daddy, I don't know nobody named Donna Gray." She began wringing her hands. Again her anxious eyes searched the boundaries of her daddy's puny living quarters.

"Honey, I guarantee you, you gonna like Donna a lot. She reminds me of your Mom some."

"Well, is she going to run off from us too, like Mom did?" Lee snapped, still avoiding eye contact.

Ed hung his head, and said nothing for a country minute. Then looking up and into her face, he said, "Lee, it's the honest to God truth that I ain't never had no luck, and I know you think I ain't been much of a daddy to you, but honey I done the best I could. Good Lord knows I tried."

Ed's voice took on an entreating tone as he continued, "Lee, I'm needing some help raising you and the other kids. You know your granny is not as fit as she used to be. Becky and Stephen are more than she can handle with her arthritis and all. Your sister, Rhonda Lynn, she ain't never gonna be no help neither. She married that soldier boy and took off like 'Snyder's pup." Being a soldier's wife is like being married to a gypsy. She don't know from one week to the next where she'll be laying down her head. Lee, honey child, I gotta have some help and that's a fact. Donna's a good woman. She's good to me and she'll be the mom to you that you never had."

Looking down again, Ed continued, "Baby, it's not easy living alone in a big city. You already know that. But, I guarantee you, Donna will treat you right. She told me time and again that she'd help me get you used to Marietta. Donna and I are expecting you to be a team player on this new deal."

Lee was out of character quiet. The furrows on her brow were now gone. She sat tall on the edge of the ugly little couch like a basketball player anxiously waiting to take the court. Wiping her sweaty hands onto the sides of her dress, she again surveyed the boundaries of the barren little apartment. Then, saying nothing, she walked to the bathroom door. Twisting the door knob and turning her body sideways, she squeezed through. Inside she saw a window. No curtains hung. Slowly she walked to the window, extended her arms, and placed her hands on the window sill. She didn't look out, but instead lowered her head and leaned forward as though pushing on the window frame. Lee wept.

———————

Tears dried and her feelings came under control. Lee reasoned a milestone had just been made in growing up. She allowed herself now to think back— back to her roots. Back to the mountains of North Georgia, where before going on to high school, she had graduated elementary school with almost a perfect attendance record. Six out of eight years she was present and on time. She recalled Granny being more proud than she was of those six curled-up certificates pinned to her bedroom wall. Each day Granny saw to it that Lee rode that yellow school bus. The bus whose sides were lined with black stripes—stripes that boldly framed the words "Epworth Elementary School."

The principal there—also her basketball coach— Robert Bell, announced the buses ready for loading at day's end without the benefit of a PA system. Strolling the halls floored with one-hundred- year old pine boards and similarly stained wainscot walls, Mr. Bell's voice thundered: "Lick Skillet, Gravely Gap, Damascus Road." This was Lee's cue. She would rise from her ancient fold-up seat whose desk surface displayed past students' carved initials, a chewed on pencil in a pencil slot, and a never-used ink well. Quick as a banty hen, she hustled down the hall to round up Becky and Stephen. Up the steps and onto the bus she led them. This team responsibility was now gone, but her sense of duty and those clay stained memories would remain.

———————

Chapter 6 - HOME IS WHERE THE HEART IS

The marriage was a tiny affair, just as Donna and Ed had agreed. Meeting and greeting strangers at a formal gathering was not what he wanted for his fifteen year old daughter. He knew that moving Lee from her mountain home and her Granny would be hard enough. In a near-empty Cobb County courthouse, with no one but Lee Ellen, Donna's sister Wanda Lou, and God witnessing the event, the justice of the peace wed Donna and Ed. Afterward there was no wedding cake, no flowers thrown over the shoulder, and no punch-drinking slow-dancing reception. A fried chicken dinner at "The Big Chicken" on Highway 41 near Lockheed Aircraft wound up the nuptials, making Ed's pockets emptier than a barn in the summer.

He was surprised and pleased as a mule eating briars to learn that Lee actually liked her step-mom. Moving to Donna's big house was the main reason. The move to her nice home went smoothly. There, Lee had privacy—something she'd never known at Granny's place with her sisters and brother.

Her stepmom was nothing like she had imagined.

Lee had expected Donna to be bossy and to restrict her freedom, but Donna forced nothing on Lee. She only required her to be ready for school, where Donna drove her each morning. Lee didn't fault Donna as a mother. It was impossible to compare her to a mother who had abandoned her. Shadowy memories were all she had of her biological mother, but still, when life seemed unfair, she sometimes thought to herself, *I wonder what having my real mom would be like?* Over time Donna earned Lee's acceptance. Teaching her to drive was the tipping point. By nature, Lee was independent and Donna knew that driving would cut the strings on her free spirit. On Saturdays, after Ed was at work, the two would slip away to a remote country road. There she learned to drive and Donna had a chance to revisit her feelings about her own coming of age. Driving would remain their shared secret. On that Georgia back road, more than anything else, Donna listened. She heard of Lee's hopes, dreams, and concerns, but never her fears. Lee would never allow anyone to know she feared anything. By simply listening, Donna earned the right to be the mom Lee had yearned for all her life.

Donna would help Lee get through the growing pains of her adolescent years. Driving the ups and downs of those old gravel roads, she left her problems in the dust. Learning to keep the car between the ditches, Lee was transformed from a North Georgia mountain girl into a big city young lady. But, adapting to the changes was not painless for either of them.

————————

"I hate this place! I hate the school and all the phony pansies, super jocks, and bony-thin model girls that go to this school. Daddy, why did you make me come down here to live? Please, let me go back to the mountains and live with Granny"

Rustling and folding the *Atlanta Constitution* he'd had his head stuck in, Ed was shocked by Lee's sudden rant. A perplexed but concerned look settled on his face. He set the newspaper aside and stared at Lee for a moment. Then in a conciliatory tone he told her, "Lee, honey child, things will get better. It'll just take some getting used to. Kinda like them new black and white Oxford shoes we got you last month. It's all part of growing up, baby. Just give it a little time."

Lee dearly loved her dad, but felt he had no idea what a day at her new school was like. He didn't know how the other students made her feel. He did not know that being a new girl in a big school some days made her feel like a stray dog lost on someone else's property.

Lee glanced at her dad and petulantly looked away, continuing her heart-felt plea, "These people in this city school don't like me. They make fun of the way I talk. You know what the other girls call me when I walk down the hall at this school? They snicker and point at me and call me Daisy May or Lo-rettie. I want to go back home, where people don't care how you talk as long as you tell the truth. Daddy, these city folks don't understand me and they're just plain mean."

"Honey, you'll get through it." Walking over to where she sat on a bean bag, he jokingly pulled at her right ear, and said, "Those other girls are just jealous of you, Lee. I bet none of them are as pretty as you at that school. That's it. They're all just green-eyed jealous."

Lee sprung to her feet like a basketball team's center. With palms up and arms held out from her side she screamed back, "You just don't know what it's like." She then lowered her head and bawled. Through wet eyes she glanced up at her dad and said, "Daddy I can't take these people at school anymore!" She then turned and fled to her bedroom, slamming the door behind her.

Shocked by Lee's out of nowhere outburst, Ed hesitated, but then hurried after her. He was stopped short by Donna who had overheard the exchange while in the kitchen. Placing a gentle hand on Ed's chest, she looked toward Lee's room and told him, "Ed, let me talk with her. This is a girl thing, and I think she will listen to me. Give me a shot, okay honey?"

"Well, if you think so. I don't know what's gotten into her. She's ill as a hornet. That's not like her."

Knocking and slowly entering Lee's room, Donna closed the door behind her, but didn't look at Lee. Instead, she fixed her eyes on a letter jacket that hung from a closet door knob. Acting coy and almost as though she had heard none of the drama between Lee and Ed, she simply asked, "Does Tommy write to you since you've moved here to Marietta?"

Like a hunting dog caught in a spring trap, Lee was ready to lash out at anyone. She snapped back with a surly response. "No...oh! Guess he thinks I dropped off the planet when I moved down here. You know what I did get, though? I got a phone call from the West Fannin football coach and he told me I had to return Tommy's jacket. Morons! Oh, I heard through the grapevine Tommy is now dating someone else. He's dating that Hawkins girl from over on Snob Row in Copperhill, Tennessee, the one that looks like Howdy Doody's sister. Guess a girl from Georgia isn't good enough for him, now. They deserve each other. She's butt-ugly and he's missing a brain!" Quick as a flash Lee flung a pillow at the jacket.

Donna, didn't respond to Lee's vent, but kept her eyes on the jacket, now swinging and swaying, but still hanging on the door knob. Then she turned to Lee and said, "Hey Lee, I have an idea. Let's go have some fun. What say we drive out to Dry Branch Road, where you practice driving? Bring that jacket with you."

Lee was stunned and speechless at first. She sniffled, looked inquisitively at Donna, but then jumped up from her bed and said, "Well..., okay. Got nothing else to do here and I need some fresh air. Let's go."

Ed had sat back down and was again engrossed in the newspaper. Leaving Lee's room, Donna yelled up the hallway to Ed, "We're going to be gone a little while. Be back in a couple of hours."

"Okay," he muttered. "I'll be right here doing what I do best." He turned the page on his newspaper and kept reading.

When they reached Dry Branch Road, it was desolate as usual—nothing in sight but acres of lonely loblolly pines and an unpicked field of corn. Out her window, Lee watched withered leaves cling precariously to tenuous corn stalks. They rose, fluttered and fell, troubled by the cool breeze.

Donna stopped the car abruptly and a cloud of road dust floated over them. A faint whistling sound from the pines was soon heard, giving Lee an uneasy feeling. She stole a searching glance at Donna who now held a thousand-yard stare at something she saw near the cornfield. She was locked onto it like she had never seen it before, but she had. Today it captured her attention. Slamming the gearshift to "park" on the steering column she ordered Lee, "Bring that jacket with you and come with me. We are going to make someone's day a little warmer." With curious skepticism Lee searched Donna's face again for a clue. *What is she up to,* she wondered. Her face revealed nothing. But her deliberate moves told Lee that her stepmom was on a mission.

Dragging the jacket on the ground, she trailed behind Donna to the cornfield's edge. Squinting into the dry wind, they stood there, quiet as mice, looking up into the blank face of a scarecrow. His body was fashioned from hay and last year's corn stalks. Tilted on his head sat a tattered straw hat. Donna's flat words surprised Lee, when she said, "Give me that jacket. He looks cold."

Donna draped and buttoned the jacket around
the scarecrow. Then she issued an order: "Come with
me. Help me gather up some of those ears of corn.
We're going to have a contest. From twenty steps
away we're going to throw corn at Mr. Glory Boy over
there in his letter jacket. The one who hits him most
times with ten throws gets a hot fudge sundae from
the Tastee Freeze back in Marietta. If he holds up long
enough, we'll make it best two-out-of-three sets. Got
any questions?"

Lee didn't have any more questions than a rabbit
would have had, but she thought, *this lady is crazy as
a coot. She doesn't even have a dog in this fight, but she
sure puts her heart into it. What could she know about
being dumped by someone?*

Quick as foxes, they piled up ears of corn for the
contest. They took turns hurling them at a target that
was for at least one of them, the object of fury. At the
end of three sets, Lee had nailed the warmly clothed
scarecrow, a.k.a. "Tommy Too Cool," a total of twenty-
three times. Hands down she won the chocolate treat.
With the mission completed, like two mercenaries they
marched back to the car. Donna, now with more pride
than anger showing on her face said to Lee, "You drive.
I'm too mad to. Next weekend we'll come back here.

If he's still wearing that ugly coat, we'll burn it. Not a word of this to anyone."

As she sat eating her trophy treat, Donna commented, "Lee, I couldn't help but notice back there in the cornfield that you have a strong throwing arm and you're doggone accurate with your throws. Ever think about playing ball for your school team?"

"No. Not really. Do... do you think I...do you think I could make the team? I played basketball at Epworth when I lived back home.

"You'll never know until you try. Why don't you talk to the coach and see when they have tryouts?"

Lee's face now shined with a wistful glow of hope. She hesitantly responded, "Okay. I may do that. First thing on lunch break Monday, I could talk to the coach." With more confidence, and speaking as though she was talking more to herself than to Donna, she said, "Yeah, think I will."

———————

Chapter 7 - THE LAST ROSE OF SUMMER

"Lee! Are you ready to go?" Donna yelled from the kitchen. "We need to leave for school. Traffic will be a turtle race this morning if we don't get ahead of it. You don't want to be late for class, do you, Honey?"

"Yes Donna, I'm almost ready," Lee yelped from her bedroom. Holding her books with one hand and a brush with the other, she marched. Echoing taps from oxfords on a wood floor told Donna that Lee was in the hallway. On a half-moon console table she dropped her books alongside an ashtray, a black rotary phone, and a worn telephone directory. Looking down the dark hall toward the kitchen, she hollered, "Give me just a minute. I want to get this rat's nest out of my hair."

Looking in the bathroom mirror at bed-mangled blonde locks, frantically she combed, removing kinks with the brush. She leaned sideways and reached low for the vanity drawer handle, grabbing out a can of hair spray. As she did, the mirror flashed an image— Granny with her thin white hair braided and neatly clasped with brown bobby pins. Lee instantly up-righted herself, paused a moment, thinking, *"Did I really just see who I think I saw?"* At first, her face set stonily in the mirror, and her eyes moistened. Then pleasant thoughts of her grandmother came to mind. A coy smile soon raced to the face of the youthful lady in the mirror.

She rejected the illusion. *My new life awaits me,* she told herself. Now seen in the mirror was only blonde hair—just the way Granny would have fixed it— straight, clean-kept, and modest. Gingerly she touched her hair and reached again for the spray. She uncapped it and created a hissing cloud above her head. Loudly snapping the cap back on, she returned it beneath the mirror. While admiring her artful creation she tilted her head from side to side and mumbled, "Tommy? I don't know anyone named Tommy."

Footsteps now tapped again on the wood floor. She hefted her books. Toward the kitchen light, down the empty hallway, her announcement resonated, "I'm ready to go."

————

The phone was ringing when Donna returned from taking Lee to school. She raced down the hall and picked up the receiver. Catching her breath she said, "Hello."

The caller said, "Hello. Is this Mrs. Bandy?"

"Yes, this is Donna. Who is calling?"

"My name is Reverend Carl Newberry, the minister at Farnswell Baptist Church in Fannin County. Is Ed there?"

"No, Ed is at work. Can I help you?"

"Well, Mrs. Bandy...Mrs. Bandy, I'm sorry to say I have some bad news. Ed's mother passed away last night. Not sure yet of the cause. She died in her sleep. The children stayed home from school this morning and some of the ladies from the church are looking after them. Could you get word to Ed? I'm sorry to have to give you this news, but we'll need Ed to come home as soon as possible. Can you get hold of him?"

"Yes. I'll call Ed at work soon as I hang up."

"Thank you Mrs. Bandy. Goodbye."

"Goodbye."

———

"Mrs. Dunaway, please send Lee Ellen Bandy to the office with her things to go home....please send Lee Ellen Bandy to the office with her things to go home." Lee's freshman English classmates stopped their work.

They raised their heads from the practice worksheet Mrs. Dunaway had given them. Listening intently, they peered at the box on the wall—the one covered with a coarse threaded tan cloth over its front and hanging near the ceiling on the classroom's front wall.

Hearing the message, each classmate randomly turned and stole a glance at Lee seated in her back row desk. Wide-eyed with disbelief she wondered, W*hy am I going back home? I just got here. Could this be some kind of a joke being played on me?*

One girl popped her gum, spun around, and winked at another girl seated across from her. Sarcastically she spoke words meant for Lee, but directed them to the entire class: "Lo-rettie, is youins killin hogs today or is youins a-pluckin chickens? Is that why yous leaving us to go home?"

A few in the class laughed loudly. Others tucked their head in shame at the hurtful sarcasm. Lee said nothing. She got up and, wearing a puckered brow, left her desk and went to the door where Mrs. Dunaway stood motioning for her to come forward. Together they stepped into the hall. The teacher then instructed her, "I don't know what this is about, but you may want to take your English book home with you. We'll be continuing in Chapter Three."

With head down, Lee re-entered the classroom to collect her things. She then dashed to her locker and retrieved all her books. On to the school office she paced.

Arriving there, she saw Donna standing outside the office door, uncharacteristically nervous and wringing her hands. Exasperated with uncertainty, Lee promptly asked, "Why are you here, Donna? Why are you taking me home?"

"I'll explain it to you later. Come with me. We'll talk in the car."

Lee followed Donna to the parking lot. Doors slammed and Donna turned her body and looked directly into Lee's face, saying, "Lee, your dad asked me to come and get you. You two are going to Blue Ridge today. He'll tell you the reason. Honey, that's all I can tell you for certain right now. Your daddy's waiting for you at home. You'll need to pack a few things to take with you."

Lee searched Donna's eyes for answers. A hint of deception or even dishonesty would be better than knowing nothing, she reasoned. In her stepmother's eyes, she saw only sadness and uncertain nothingness. Her face was like the last rose of summer—trying hard, but failing to look as though the future was bright. Lee looked out the window. She said nothing on her quick trip to join her waiting dad.

The sky was a wet gray and a cold soppy mist coated the windshield. The worn wipers worked double time, half smearing and half removing the recurring mixture of rain and then drizzle from the car's fogged up windshield. Lee's bitter words burst out as she wiped tears from her trembling cheeks: "Why Daddy? Why did God take Granny away? Don't He know we need Granny here?"

Ed was not a man prone to tears, but he looked like he was fixing to cry. Fighting back tears, in a defeated yet consoling tone he answered, "Lee, I don't know why God took Mom. No one knows what kilt Mom. The coroner said she died in her sleep—probably from a heart attack. Said she just went out like a light bulb in the middle of the night, and that she didn't suffer any. We can thank God for that."

Ed and Lee Ellen were on their way to Blue Ridge and it was a long ways off. Ninety-three miles north,

Granny's body lay at rest. It would be a long trip.

Georgia Highway 5, a narrow, middle-lined curvy road with few straight-a-ways was the road traveled. The trip time was normally about two and one-half hours, but rain would make this trip longer. Traffic light stops in several small towns made driving time unpredictable.

Each town also had railroad crossings. A stop at a train crossing could delay traffic for fifteen minutes. The towns included Woodstock, Canton, Jasper, Elijay, Blue Ridge, and finally McCaysville, where the Lark Funeral Home was located. Granny's body lay there in rest.

Woodstock came first. Keenum's Drugstore was a landmark of sorts for Lee. It was on the left, just after a railroad crossing. Seeing the store once gave Lee a sense of belonging when she first moved from the mountains. She knew Mike Keenum, the store owner's nephew. At Epworth he and Lee had attended school together. Today neither the familiar name nor anything else had meaning. She thought about nothing but her Granny.

Canton, a mill town with several traffic lights was next. A large cotton mill lay alongside Highway 5 and the musty smell of cotton dust permeated the air. Lee smelled nothing today.

Jasper, a town with one red light, one caution light, and a bridge over the railroad tracks was next. Snuff-dipping men sometimes hunkered down on their heels on the sidewalk. On Sunday, men in suits with bad ties lined the fronts of closed stores. All scrutinized motorists passing through Jasper. Lee saw no one today in Jasper.

Ellijay always gave Lee hope that the trip to the mountains was nearly over. Her mountains lay ahead. Ed was concerned that Lee, so far, had said nothing the whole trip. He turned toward her, nodded his head toward a school house, and asked, "Do you remember playing Ellijay in basketball last year in that gym?"

Lee remained mute. She could hear nothing but the sound of Granny humming "I'll Fly Away" She then burst into bitter tears.

No longer could Ed control his own feelings of hurt and loss and sorrow. He pulled the car to the side of the road and immediately wept violently. Together in the pounding rain, they wept in solitude. Cars noisily passed them by, splashing waves from puddles against their car.

Regaining his composure, Ed looked at Lee who now had stopped crying, but appeared to be in a daze. He softly said, "Lee, Mom's in a better place now. She done something all of us will have to do some day. Today, you and I got to get through this. There're other folks who are depending on you and me to be strong. We've got some things we got to get done at the funeral home and I need for you to be strong for me and keep it together for Becky and Stephen. Your brother Ray, he ain't going to get to come home for the funeral. That's the problem with being in the army— they only allow you to leave duty for funerals of your next of kin. And, your older sister Rhonda Lynn, she's not going to be any help. Well, you know how she is. She ain't all there sometimes. She's all grown up and married, but still she acts like a kid ever now and then. So, Lee, I need your help. Can I depend on you, Honey, to keep it together? There'll be time later for you to cry. Right now, we got to show some strength. You're the strongest kid I got, Lee. You can do it. I know you can."

"O.K. Daddy. I'll try, but it's not gonna be easy."

Chapter 8 - OLD FORDS AND YOUNG PROMISES

The cloud-blocked sun had slanted low when they arrived at the old home place. A few cars were parked out front. A rocking chair swayed, slowly seesawing on the plain-boarded porch that skirted the house. Granny had loved to sit out there, rocking the grandchildren, listening to frogs in late spring and the katydids in early autumn. She'd retire there on hot summer mornings after she'd worked in her garden. This evening the porch was cold, gloomy, and foreboding.

In the house, woodstove smoke, mixed with the smell of fried chicken filled the air. Church people had brought in the customary funeral food. In the living room on a couch, sat Lee's younger brother and sister. Their feet stuck straight out and they stared into space with question marks on their face. Two ladies from the church sat nearby in ladder-back chairs. They were there to sit up with the dead. Even though Granny's body rested seven miles north at Lark's Funeral Home, it was a tradition which mountain people refused to let go. Wet wood crackled in the stove, but no one heard it or felt its heat.

Hearing the screen door close and then seeing Lee enter the front door, the children looked up and sprang to their feet. Quiet little eyes studied her face. They sought answers to the same questions Lee herself had.

The older sister, Rhonda Lynn was also there. Muttering meaningless words she dragged her shoes on the linoleum floor as she flitted about the house. She blathered on and on about irrelevant concerns: "Why did the church send all that food? Who's going to eat all this? When am I supposed to return the dishes?" To the family, Rhonda Lynn's questions made as much sense as anything else. Since Granny's passing, nothing seemed relevant. Each family member felt confused, lost, and as disoriented as a blind mule in a hail storm.

After sampling some of the funeral food, Ed and Lee tucked the children into bed. As best they could, they answered their questions about death. They consoled their hurt, their fears, and their angst that hung heavy in this remote mountain home that no longer felt the same. In the morning the funeral arrangements would be made by Ed and Lee.

———————

Lark Funeral Home was a Fannin County landmark. It more resembled a rambling ranch style house than a funeral home. Soft light shimmered from its large picture window where a lampshade stayed on both day and night. Architecturally and artistically, it was a thing of beauty.

Lush hollies lined the white trimmed façade and an immaculately kept lawn encircled the building. It set back parallel to the road—Georgia Highway 5— the road they had traveled, that dead-ended at the red light in McCaysville. A left turn there and you were promptly in Copperhill, Tennessee.

The raw, nasty weather from the day before had moved on. The rain had stopped. It had turned cold and a brisk wind stirred with the sun now trying to peek out from behind the clouds. Ed and Lee pulled into a mostly empty large space at Lark's—a parking lot abundantly covered with small pristine stones. They were round and bright white. Two shiny black rain-dotted hearses and an old eggshell-colored, rusted-out Ford sedan were in clear view.

The old Ford's body was typical of the area. Its fenders were dented, eaten-out, and flimsy as chicken wire. Sulfuric acid, a corrosive chemical from the nearby Tennessee Copper Company, was the evil doer. The plant's acid rain environment was a cancer to fenders. Any car entering the plant was exposed to this hazard with its delayed consequences. Work cars belonging to the company's employees all suffered varying degrees of the disease.

As Ed and Lee exited their car, they heard a grinding screech coming from the old Ford. With his head bowed, a young bearded man slammed its door and adjusted his faded blue jeans. Leisurely, he trailed them to a canopy-covered side entrance. Together the three entered and stood in a dimly lit lobby area. The fragrance was striking—that of carnations and roses and an unknown disinfectant. The odor was loud, pungent, and onerous. The owners, Robert Lark and Sheldon, his son, were not around and the place was quiet as a cave. Breaking the somberness and making his presence known, the young man spoke up.

"Mr. Bandy?"

"Oh, hey Jimmy," said Ed half-heartedly, spinning around while rubbing his eyes. "It is Jimmy Satterfield isn't it?"

"Yep, that's me. You remembered me! I'm surprised. It's been a while." He then half-closed his mouth, breathed in air through his front teeth, making a hissing sound.

"Sorry I didn't recognize who you were at first. That morning sun bouncing off the white gravel kind of blinded me. How are you doing?"

Lee nodded her head at the young man, listened intently, but did not make eye contact.

"I'm doing fine Mr. Bandy." Jimmy then paused. In a remorseful, albeit rehearsed tone he said with deepest sincerity, "I sure was saddened to hear of your mom's passing. She was a fine lady. Yes siree. No better liked person here in Fannin County." Again, he hissed air through his front teeth.

"Well, thank you for those kind words, Jimmy. Yes, she was well thought of in this community." Things got silent and Ed wondered, "What is he doing here? He's not blood related to my folks."

Looking about, Ed said, "Jimmy, we are here to make some arrangements for Mom's funeral, but it looks like everyone is gone. Wonder where they are?"

In a matter-of-fact knowing way, Jimmy quickly asserted, "Oh, they're here. One of them is always here. They'll be around in a minute or two." Sucking air again, he delayed a moment and said, "Could...could we talk just briefly before they show up, Mr. Bandy?"

"Sure. What is this about?"

"Well, let's step outside under the canopy a minute so we can talk in private," Jimmy said as he motioned toward the door with his head.

"Lee, you wait here," Ed said. "I'll be right back. If anyone shows up, tell them we are here to make arrangements and then you come outside and get me. Okay?"

Lee nodded affirmative and remained silent. She cut her eyes at Jimmy as they exited. Vaguely she recalled Jimmy once being a friend of her older brother Ray, but she had not seen him since Ray joined the army over a year back. His hair was shorter then, he had no beard, and that spaced-out look in his eyes was not there. Like the Queen's castle guard, Lee stood at attention, waiting for the owner.

"Mr. Bandy, I'll get right to the point. I called your Mom's home and they told me I might find you here. I know you don't have time to kill. There are two things I need to speak with you about and neither will take much time. The first is sort of hard to say and I know this ain't the best of times, but I thought it might be my only time to speak with you about it. You live way down yonder in Alana now, don't you?"

"Yes, Jimmy. That's right. I moved down there a while back. Right after Rhonda Lynn got married and

Ray joined the army."

Nervously, Jimmy brushed and tugged at his beard, pushed back his hair, trying to order his thoughts. He then proceeded with his first question. "Well you see Mr. Bandy, Ray cut out of here owing me money. When he left town, he didn't come by and pay me like he said he would. You see, Ray and me both got thrown in jail one night by Sheriff Massey. We'd been drinking a little, and I bet Ray ten dollars he couldn't climb across the top of the Ocoee Bridge down there by Ralph and Grady's Beer Joint. Well, he tried it, but we both got arrested before he made it to the top of the bridge. Sheriff Massey told him "You come down from the bridge or I'll shoot you down deader than a possum." Ray didn't want to lose the bet, but he had no choice. Sheriff took us both in. We spent the night together in the Fannin County Jail. They released us the next morning on our own recognizance, but there was money to be paid to the court. Uncle Royce came up to the courthouse and squared everything for me and Jimmy. So, Ray is all square with the court now, but you see, he never did pay me back so I can't pay back Uncle Royce the fifty dollars he's owed for getting us out of jail. I thought maybe you'd like to make good on what Ray owes me." Again, with refined humility, Jimmy looked compassionately at Ed and told him,

"Now, Mr. Bandy, I ain't got no way of getting hold of Ray. I heard tell he was overseas in that Vietnam War. You know, he may not make it back, and I sure do need my money." Jimmy shut his mouth, paused a second, and then hissed more air in through his teeth.

Pain, disappointment, and dismay dripped from Ed's face. He looked at Jimmy, but said nothing.

Jimmy switched back to his all-business tone. He continued, "Now, I don't expect my winnings on that bet. I honestly believe Ray would have crossed that bridge had the sheriff not threatened to shoot him down, but I'd be much obliged if you'd consider paying me back the money Jimmy owes me. I sure could use it."

Ed squinted out at the sun glaring off the white stoned parking lot. The sun was nearing its noon position, but the air was cool. Suddenly the Tennessee Copper Company's eleven o'clock dinner-whistle blew. He shook his head, stuck his index finger in his right ear, and fiercely shook it. Looking at Jimmy again he snapped, "And what was the other thing about?"

"Well, it's about what you are here for today. You see, I work for Edmonds' Cemetery Supply in Blue Ridge. I don't know if you knew that or not.

Anyway, I wanted to let you know that Mr. Edmonds
told me to tell you he could give you a good deal on
your choice of a fine tombstone for Mrs. Bandy. Its
price would be a lot less than what you'll pay anyone
else. They're all hand polished and engraved with up
to eighty-seven characters at no charge. You won't find
a better tombstone in North Georgia, I guarantee it.
All Edmonds' tombstones come straight from Elberton.
It's the granite capital of the world, you know. Ain't no
better tombstone in the world than one from Elberton,
Georgia. You'll get real value out of an Elberton
tombstone. So, Mr. Edmonds would appreciate it if
you'd keep him in mind. Come by Blue Ridge and pick
one out, why don't you? He'll do you right. He's a fine
man, Mr. Edmonds. Yes siree."

Ed's head tottered and his thinning hair began
to quiver as a gust of cold air swept by. His jerking
hand reached for his back pocket to remove his wallet.
Fumbling nervously, his mouth twisted in stern
concentration as he removed two twenties and a ten
dollar bill. Handing them to Jimmy, he looked into
his eyes and in a quavering voice told him, "Jimmy, I
think Mr. Lark will be handling the tombstone needs.
I'll come by if he doesn't. It's chilly out here. Think I'll
go back inside."

Jimmy accepted the money, stuck it in his front pocket, and said, "Thank you Mr. Bandy. I'm truly sorry for your loss. I'll be praying for you and your family." Quick as a scared rabbit, he turned and hot-footed across the round white stones.

Ed stood dazed and reflective. Wistfully he watched Jimmy's every step, much like a crazed-dog watches chickens pecking the ground. With his opened wallet unknowingly held to his side he stood stunned as though he had just seen someone's dank doom revealed or maybe his own ghost from a past life. His face had turned white as a sheet and a look of wounded woe and wonderment settled on him.

As he lit a cigarette with one hand, he could see the raggedy-ass youngster get in the old rusted-out car. Ed's hearing was never more acute. He clearly heard the car's starter grind, struggling to crank the engine and then pop when it caught on and started. He could hear its worn tires crunch the white gravel as it crept toward the blacktop. He heard, but ignored piercing blasts from its hole-ridden muffler. It coughed. It sputtered. A blue haze clouded about it when it stopped to turn right at the blacktop. As it gained speed on Highway 5, he heard the clashing gears growl and groan and saw each new blue cloud trail and rise each time Jimmy up-shifted. Ed heard it all. Soon it was out of sight, but he could still hear the old car; hugging the high ground, toward Blue Ridge it clattered, rumbled, and rolled along. The sounds were echoes from his past, a weightless memory that floated in to haunt him each time he returned to his mountains.

He smoked his cigarette down to a nub and then snuffed it out on his shoe sole. He stuck the nub in his shirt pocket, looked up, and gave a troubled glance at the fast passing clouds. He stuck his wallet in his back pocket, turned, and walked back inside to join Lee.

———————

Chapter 9 - THE PRICE OF DYING

"Hey honey. Has anyone shown up yet?"

"Nope," Lee blurted out in frustration. "Where are they?" Pointing at a small silver bell suspended from a nearby door frame she said, "I thought about ringing that bell, but I was not certain what might happen if I did."

"Let's give it a try," Ed said in a winsome voice as he stepped toward the doorway. He reached his hand for the tiny bell and gave it several fast clangs.

Sheldon Lark was a symbol of the morose atmosphere of death. Stolid faced and having no distinctive features other than resembling everyone's forgotten first cousin, he was still somehow personable and even engaging. He was a natural born undertaker, having followed in his dad's footsteps. A tolling bell had been his family's dance song for now over half a century. Today this trite little man would again revel in defeating death's chaos, help pick up the pieces, and restore order to another train wreck of jumbled emotions.

His heavily starched white shirt crinkled and the

limp bland, unclipped necktie he wore fell forward as he leaned and reached his hand to greet Ed. "Hello. Sorry if I kept you folks waiting. I was busy in the back," he said as he stroked back his prematurely receding hair with his other hand. "How can I help you?"

"Well, Mr. Lark, I'm Ed Bandy and this is my daughter Lee Ellen. We're here to see about making arrangements for Mom's...." Ed choked up. He looked away at the small silver bell he had rung. Hearing his own words articulate the fact of his mom's demise was now real for the first time. He continued, "We would like your help in picking out a nice burial plan for Mom."

Humble as a robin on a windowsill, Sheldon tilted his torso, solemnly bowed his head, and closed his big brown eyes. Keeping his upper body tilted, he then opened them and spoke in a mournful tone, "Mr. Bandy, these are trying times. It's a real strain on you. We'll do everything we can to make services for your mom as easy on you and the family as we know how."

Ed was not a man known for sentimental self-pity, but the words cut him to the heart. He cupped his hands over his face and briskly paced away a few steps. There he leaned against a dark hallway wall and wept. Lee was more surprised than saddened by her dad's never before seen display of grief. Her life-long image of her dad was a man tough as a pine knot, giving in to nothing, and never shedding a tear. She looked at Sheldon and dryly said, "Give us just a minute, please."

"Certainly, young lady; I'll be right there in that office when y'all are ready," he said, nodding his balding head toward the small silver bell. Keeping his body slightly bowed and with no more presence than a fly on the wall, he was gone.

Ed soon pulled himself together. He blew his nose and shoved his hanky in his back pocket. Then he primly walked toward the office, not acknowledging Lee, as she followed close behind him. Entering the office doorway with his jaw set and his fists clenched, he addressed Sheldon, "Okay, I think I'm ready to get on with this, now."

"Fine. Fine. Fine," muttered Sheldon. "You folks come on in and have a seat."

"Mr. Lark, you know my family. We ain't rich, but we want mom to have a nice funeral. I don't want nothing cheap."

"Sure Mr. Bandy. You want a respectable service truly worthy of the example your mom set for us all. Dignified, am I right about that?"

"Well, yes. That's about it. We don't want anything sorry looking and I don't want a bunch of flowers on her... coffin. Just simple, but ... yes, respectable is what I'd like."

"Sure. Sure. Sure. I think I know exactly what you have in mind. We call it our "Heaven's Dove" plan. It's an all-in-one plan. Everything is included. We take care of everything, even the tombstone."

Looking more attentive, Ed looked up and asked, "Well, how much does something like that go for? You see, I'm a little stretched for money."

"Well, Mr. Bandy, the price is tolerable. We have more expensive plans, but you have told me that's not what you'd like. You don't want gobs of flowers, and I don't blame you. This plan will give you..."

"How much money are we talking about here, Mr. Lark?" Ed interrupted.

"Well, with Georgia's excise taxes and everything, it would run you... Here, let me check it for sure for you on this machine and then we'll know exactly how much it will be."

Ed interjected another question as Sheldon turned toward an old adding machine with a long hand crank on it. "Now it'll be a nice one, won't it? We want more than just a pine box for...Mama." Tears again welled up in Ed's eyes. Softly Sheldon set in front of Ed a box of tissues, but Ed rejected the offer. He sniffed hard, twisted his face, and reached defiantly for his back pocket, saying, "I got my own hanky right here, thank ye."

"Fine. Fine. Fine." Shelton turned back around and began entering numbers into the long handled adding machine. Each time he cranked the handle, a clicking clangor was made and Ed's eyebrows raised, but he said nothing.

Meticulously Sheldon tore off the paper tape from the adding machine. He tiptoed around his desk and handed the printout to Ed. He said in an almost angelic voice, "Mr. Bandy, for our Heaven's Dove plan, it would be only eight hundred and seventeen dollars and twenty-three cents. Now that includes our Fannin County resident's discount. Here at Lark, you don't have to pay them high Tennessee sales taxes. If the burial takes place anywhere in Fannin County, we give you back four percent of the total cost. You can't go wrong with this plan, Mr. Bandy. It's the best value we have to offer." Sheldon gently bowed his head and stepped back while Ed perused the numbers on the small strip of paper.

"Could we see a picture of the coffin?" Ed asked without looking up.

"We can do better than that, Mr. Bandy. You just follow me. I'd be more than happy to show y'all our elegant casket." Sheldon cut his deadpan eyes toward the silver bell over the doorway and said, "Come with me"

Together the three meandered through the maze of the deceptively spacious building until they came to a set of double doors. Sheldon opened one door, flipped a switch, and whispered, "Come on in. Come right on in." As though the sun had just come up, illumination saturated the room, showcasing about a dozen opened coffins. Each was morbidly silent, yet each had an unabashed attitude and an alluring appeal—proud, distinguished, and deserving of attention.

Standing at one's end, Sheldon folded his hands over his stomach, stood erect, and gave a confident tight-lipped smile. He hesitate a second and then said, "This is the "Heaven's Dove" coffin." Like light reflecting off a broken mirror's scattered pieces, glints and beams bounced from the coffin's long chrome-coated handles. The lining was luxurious lavender velvet. Sheldon's smile suddenly diminished and he demurely said, "I have to say, I think it's the best of the lot. Of course, I'm sort of partial to this one because it is my own design. My patent's pending for it, but it's just a matter of time...Just a matter of time until it's approved." He then turned, looked away, and wryly asked, "What do y'all think of this finely crafted piece?"

Keeping her distance, Lee furrowed her brow and skeptically peered at the coffin. Ed took slow steps toward the coffin. He stroked the smooth stained woodwork and felt the velvet door lining. He then turned to Sheldon and said, "I think this here is what we're looking for."

"Good choice, Mr. Bandy, good choice," said Sheldon. "You have made the right decision. You won't go wrong with that coffin. I guarantee it's well worth every cent. It's becoming our most popular one."

Quickly, they returned to the front of the building. They walked under the small silver bell and entered the office. There, Ed signed the agreement and counted out three hundred dollars in cash from his wallet, and handed it to Sheldon. The remainder would be paid within one month following the burial date, November 29, 1966.

Ed and Lee promptly returned to the old home place.

———————

Chapter 10 - DO NOT STAND AT MY GRAVE

Do not stand at my grave and weep

I am not there; I do not sleep.

I am a thousand winds that blow,

I am the diamond glints on snow,

I am the sun on ripened grain,

I am the gentle autumn rain.

When you awaken in the morning's hush

I am the swift uplifting rush

Of quiet birds in circled flight.

I am the soft stars that shine at night.

Do not stand at my grave and cry,

I am not there; I did not die.

- Mary E. Frye

The News Observer obituary column reported the funeral to be a private ceremony, attended only by family members, but that was not exactly true. In attendance for the funeral of Ethel Viola Stiles Bandy—better known as Granny Bandy—were numerous others. Several not attending had sent wreaths, ferns, and potted plants with attached condolence cards.

Rhonda Lynn's sister-in-law and her six stair-step children all attended the funeral. They all wore their good church clothes. On two full pews they sat with Rhonda Lynn with her two much younger boys. The older boys were not well-behaved. They snickered, squirmed around in the pews, and sneaked jabs and pinches at each other. The oldest boy pretended to pick his nose and flip buggers. Their rascally antics angered the daughter-in-law. She spun around in her pew, scowled at the boys. When she saw the two little girls beside them cringing, she then slapped at them.

Several ladies from the church, including the ones who had sat up with the family after Granny died, were there as well. They sat on the back rows of the church, as stiff as sticks of stove wood. With righteous, leathery faces they cut skeptical eyes at all who entered the church. One was heard to inquire: "How old was she? Did they ever tell what kilt her?" When one well-dressed lady entered the services all alone, another was heard to gab, "That's Rose Ella, Grady Grindstaff's daughter, by his first wife. You know, I heard tell she married a deaf man." To which another with tight lips glibly lamented, "They's all deaf, don't ye know?—men."

Granny had no brothers or sisters attending. They were all deceased. She and her older siblings were born and raised "down below the mountains" in

Etowah, Tennessee. Granny had moved to Fannin County when her husband, Luther, got on at the copper company working in the mines. They couldn't get a company house so they rented a little shot-gun house from Ruth Goldberg. Later they bought the old farm house, which Luther fixed up. Luther died a young man. He was killed in a mining accident and his body could not be recovered. The Heaven's Dove tombstone would, however, include both his and Granny's names, dates of birth, and dates of death.

Ed's estranged and out-of-town brother, Tom, barely made it in time for the noon services. He'd flown in from Dallas, Texas. In Chattanooga he rented a car, drove the Old Copper Road, and arrived at the old home place about two hours shy of starting time.

Tom was nothing like Ed. Ten years Ed's senior, he had a voracious appetite for money, and saw no way to whet his appetite in the mountains of North Georgia. After a stint in the military, an army buddy encouraged him to go into the real estate business. "He'd done good," in Dallas as the mountain locals were fond of saying about others who had "left the country."

Before the services at the family gathering at the old home place, Tom didn't fail to let the others know just how well he'd done. Yet he did not ask about nor offer to help pay for the Heaven's Dove funeral service. Tom asked only if Granny had made out a will and who was the executor. When told "No," he promptly walked to his rental car, placed a call on its watts-line, and made arrangements for a same evening flight back to Dallas.

Sheldon was a maestro and a credit to his profession. He brought great order, respect, and decorum to the ceremony. "All please stand," he commanded the congregants. Behind his lead marched the pallbearers. Like drilled soldiers, they manned and guided the casket down the center aisle from the church's only entrance. The flower-covered coffin at the front of the little church loomed large. It was almost majestic and upstaged the young slim preacher sheltered behind the podium. He softly said, "Let us pray."

His quavering voice brought a brief message. It followed a hector-bell soprano's scratchy rendition of "I Come to The Garden Alone." A simple ceremony was what Ed had wanted and simple was what the attendees got. No graveside services followed the benediction. Oddly, mourning groans or bitter crying were not heard during the services. All outward grieving was gone.

The pallbearers rolled the casket to the rear entrance. The small crowd then stood respectfully silent. They peered around the flower-scented church with questioning looks forming on their faces as if to say, "What just happened here? Is Granny Bandy really gone?"

Twelve hands gripped and lifted the chrome handled Heaven's Dove. Into the hearse it rolled and slid. The rear door slammed shut and the hearse followed by the pallbearers, crept to the adjacent cemetery.

Gracefully, but hurriedly, the bereaved retreated—all adjourned to the old home place. There they indulged in the sumptuous dinner prepared by the ladies of the church. They enjoyed each other's company, exchanged quiet conversion, but none spoke of the dearly departed. It was as if she had never existed. All the memories of Granny became private.

Chapter 11 - ALL NET

Lee took to the court like a duck takes to pond water. Basketball was the eye of the storm she'd ride to the other side of her turbulent teen years. Her stepmom had not steered her wrong as Lee suspected at first. Donna had not pandered her to gain acceptance when she told her she had potential and advised her to go out for the team. Lee's innate skepticism had been misdirected, but she soon made amends with Donna and trusted her.

She was not totally new to the game. In the mountains she played for Epworth, but rarely saw game-time and this angered her. There, Lee's height was at odds with the coach's strategy—"feed the ball to the tall girls near the hoop to shoot." That strategy won games for one reason only: Epworth had a herd of Amazon girls. Unlike Lee, their speed was glacier slow and their shots hit the basket less often than Helen Keller's would have. Poor shooting did have a benefit: it made the forwards good rebounders. Lee's passing, dribbling, and ball handling came along nicely, but she lacked passion for the game. These were all essential for playing contemporary girls' half-court basketball.

The sport served Lee well for several reasons. It gave her an acceptable outlet for her repressed anger. Her anger was transformed to passion for the game. The chip she'd carried on her shoulder was slowly whittled away. The trash hand dealt her in life's game was the culprit. Her mom had abandoned her; she was forced from her small mountain community into a concrete jungle inhabited by unfamiliar and seemingly selfish people; her grandmother, the only mother figure she had ever known, had un-expectantly died. These all made Lee feel justified in her bitter attitude.

She changed and learned valuable lessons for life from the uncompromising teachings of basketball. From this dean of discipline, she got to know herself maybe better than she ever wanted to. No longer did she hide inside her former small-eyed world. Basketball forced her to broaden her horizons and to face challenges head-on. Those challenges seemed harsh—harsher than falling while racing barefooted down a graveled mountain road. In the beginning she found it all more repulsive than two dogs fighting, but she learned from its ugly demands—they made her tough as nails.

She came to know the truth of her limits, her temperament, and her new surroundings. Most importantly, she learned to admit her feelings, and voice them. While treading the murky waters of sports, she caught sight of who she could become in life if only she set goals, took risks, and worked hard. She questioned the validity of her up-to-now viewpoint. Conversing with strangers, trusting her teammates and others, would be new. Collaborating, she learned, was the key to winning at this game she came to love. Her familiar old friend, bad luck, would not go away. Conflict would be Lee's constant companion and the agent of change through her coming of age.

———

"You can take it and shove it where the sun doesn't shine," she said, hurling her Sibley High School team uniform in his face. His eyebrows raised and shock flooded his eyes—almost more than any of the backup players who heard her words over the hum of the filled gym. The stunned apple-faced coach with the crew-cut hair removed the sweaty uniform that hung from his head and shoulders. He managed to spit out only two words, "What's wrong?"

The starting team didn't see what happened. They were huddled near the scorekeeper's bench waiting for the horn to blow that would send them to the court for the second half's start. But the scene was not missed by the Sibley High crowd. They also saw the player come into the stands and take a seat with her equally astonished parents.

Coach Bender was a winning coach, but he had a flaw. He could not stop himself from riding a player. Habitually during a game—win or lose—he would single out one player, would bird-dog that player, and would run up and down the court bawling out the player. Tonight, at the end of the first half, his ranting was cut short.

He had lost a good player. Jane Goodwin was not a clutch player, but was dependable and full of hustle. Tonight in a critical game between juggernauts Sibley High and Maddox High, Goodwin's basketball career would end and Lee's would begin.

Goodwin knew she would not start the second half. Coach Bender had already made that clear to Goodwin during the locker room pep-talk. The daughter of Sibley Board of Education member, Herschel Henderson, would get the nod to replace Goodwin to start the second half of this tied game.

Nancy Henderson was tall, but not physical, and she played the game like a prim badminton player. Much of her game time was spent rearranging her long straight ponytail and fluttering her hands at her side.

Two minutes into the second half, the buzzer blared and the referee stopped the game. Henderson was face down on the court, crying with a palm cupped over her left eye. An accidental eye-poke froze the game and a referee helped her to the bench. Coach Bender needed another substitute, but his backup bench's depth was paper-thin. He rubbed the back of his tense neck with his hand as he paced the sideline studying his slim player choices.

After glimpsing at the scoreboard, his gaping eyes cut to the bench. Looking at no one in particular, with a catty tone he ordered, "Bandy, *you*. Get in there. Take Henderson's place."

Lee's eyes popped open wider than if she'd seen a copperhead snake. She thought her ears had failed her and doubted what she had heard. *Could this be?"* she asked herself. *I'm only a sophomore and Coach wants me to go into a varsity game!* Nervously biting her fingernail, she pointed with her other hand's index finger back at herself. She then found courage to voice a question to the stressed out coach, "Me, coach? You want *me* to go in?"

Twirling his right hand as he sprinted toward the substitute bench, he nodded his head up and down, and barked at Lee, the other substitutes, and a silent waiting crowd, "Yes *you*, stupid. Get down there to the scorekeeper and get checked in."

Lee sprang to her feet and dashed to the scorekeeper's bench, still not believing this to be for real. The buzzer sounded and she took her place on the court. Two tall girls from opposing teams faced each other at midcourt. The referee hefted the ball above them and the second half began.

The tipped off ball twisted and took a weird corkscrew direction toward Sibley High's end of the court. Like a shortstop, Lee scooped up the ball and without bouncing it she fired it to a forward standing alone in the paint. It was a short free-throw and two easy points—points scored in less than five seconds. The coach called time out and took Lee out of the game. He sent in a taller, senior girl to replace Lee.

The game with Maddox High dragged on and Sibley trailed by five points most of the game, but now trailed by two. Thirty seconds remained in the game when the referee blew his whistle. Sibley's point leader had fouled out. A new player was needed.

Again Coach Bender looked dejectedly at his substitutes. "Alright Bandy, get back in there," he said as a trickle of pessimistic fans begun filing toward the exit. The buzzer sounded and Lee took the court. She readied herself for the ball to be returned to her forwards' end of the court following Maddox's double bonus free throw attempts.   Both free throws were missed.

The second free throw was rebounded by Sibley's guard. Quickly she threw the ball to another guard, who was pressed hard. After eight seconds had ticked off the clock, the guard managed to get the ball across the center line into Lee's hands.

As practiced, Lee brought the ball up to the key and looked for another forward to pass the ball to. Both the other two forwards were covered like white on rice. Lee too, was hovered over by an all-arms tall girl who prevented a clear throw. The waning seconds of this game ticked off the clock, as she continued to dribble, searching for a way to evade her defender. The pick play her team had practiced did not develop. No open line of fire to the forward came open either. With one second showing on the clock, Lee faded back and quickly hurled a lofty hook shot from behind the key. The buzzer blared as the ball traveled. It was an all net shot! The buzzer continued even after the ball cleared the net, but no points were registered on the scoreboard. The Sibley crowd stood up and began murmuring, waiting for maybe a stuck score board to be corrected, the tying two points registered, and the beginning of an overtime period to begin. It did not happen.

Coach Bender raced to the scorekeeper's bench demanding an explanation. He was told "the game clock had expired before the ball cleared the shooter's hand. Your shooter did not get her shot off in time."

Coach Bender's face got redder than a cayenne pepper and his short stubbly graying hair appeared to bristle like a porcupine. All hell was about to break loose, or so the crowd thought. Flailing his arms he got right in a referee's face, bobbling his head and screaming. All the things he screamed were of no relevance to the game, however, but the crowd was certain a score change was forthcoming. Coach Bender knew different. As a veteran coach, he knew that referees never change their mind once they'd made a call. His crowd pleasing drama changed nothing on the scorekeeper's ruling.

The Sibley High crowd booed and jeered at the referees. Balled up popcorn bags and paper cups were hurled onto the court. The early exiting folks turned around, froze, waiting to learn what they had missed. In less than a minute, the score board was turned off, court lights were dimmed, and the referees slipped out the back door.

———————

The game was logged in Sibley High's "L" column. Lee's team had failed to make it to the regional playoff due to losing this last game of the season to Maddox High. The breakeven season would soon be forgotten. Coach Bender was encouraged to resign—he was not aware that the uniform-slinging girl who quit the team was the daughter of the county's local newspaper editor. But the Sibley students and fans would not forget Lee's beat-the-buzzer shot and the questionable time call by the referee.

———————

Chapter 12 - FREE DREAMS

When Lee arrived at school on Monday morning, she thought Donna had delivered her to the wrong school. Smiling faces greeted her in the hallway. Students congratulated her: "Great shot Bandy!" "Those refs need glasses and some Ex-Lax. You're my hero Bandy!" "We'll get that Maddox Trash next year."

Even her Geometry teacher, Mr. Gibson, gave her a compliment.   "Perfect trajectory you placed on that ball, Bandy. Perfect!" For the first time since moving from the mountains, Lee felt like a valuable human being, someone whom others looked up to. But, like her favorite poet Emily Dickenson, she knew fame was a fickle food and memories quickly slid away. Her basketball experience would take a major direction change in her junior year.

In 1967 Atlanta area high schools began integrating. Some all-black schools were shut down and their students joined previously all-white schools. In the fall season, 1966-67, for the first time ever, Lee interacted with blacks, both on and off the basketball court.

————

"Hey...Darlene," Jim whispered as he turned in his desk. He then flipped and landed a neatly folded note on her desk and whispered again, "Pass that back to Lee." Sibley High's starting quarterback then nodded his above-the-crowd head toward the back. Lee had tuned out the whispers. She focused on the chalkboard. There, meticulously, Mr. Gibson drew a triangle and the proof to the Pythagorean Theorem. The note's travel went unseen by few in the back half of the class where mostly black students sat.

On top of Lee's open text book the note now lay unattended. At first Lee looked at the note like it was a sleeping dog. Cutting her eyes about, she tried to see who was looking. To the disappointment of her spectators, quick as a blue jay she lifted the note and tucked it between the back pages of her opened Geometry book. The last thing she wanted was to be embarrassed in class.

Mr. Gibson turned and began, "Today you will be introduced to one of the most used theorems of the modern world. You will be expected not only to know this theorem, but also to logically prove its validity. This theorem is fundamental to everything we will do for the remainder of the year. So I highly recommend that you pay attention."

Lee tried to listen and concentrate, but Mr. Gibson might as well have been teaching a telephone pole. She squirmed in her desk like she was sitting on rusty fishhooks; she fidgeted with the pleats on her jumper skirt and tugged at her knee socks. Floating in the back of her mind was the note. She had about two hundred and ninety-seven concerns about that note. Tilting her head down, a veiled mystic smile appeared, lingered, but was then missing from her face. She was back in the mountains and recalled: *I once got a note from that shy boy at Epworth. It began, 'I like you. Do you like me? Please check in the box. Yes or No.' I checked Yes, sent it back to him, and he read it. His two big ears turned red and he never did talk to me again. Boys! They are all crazy.* Somberness next found her face. Serious as a heart-attack she thought: I*t could be worse than that. Maybe one of these black girls doesn't like me. Maybe it's the short fat blackberry-black one or maybe that tall light-skinned one— the one with the cocked blue eyes that's all the time looking at my eyes. Maybe one of them wants to fight me. That note may be telling me where I'm to meet her to get my next public assistance can of whip-ass.*

At the end of class, Lee remained at her desk as others filed out of the class. Quick as a chicken chasing a June bug she grabbed the note and read it.

It simply said, "Will you go with me to the Easy Glider Roller Rink on Saturday?" She looked up and saw Jim smiling at her. He then lifted his lanky body from his desk and swaggered toward her. An unfamiliar fear swept over her. Her palms got sweaty and she felt queasy. "Well, will you go? Some of the guys from the football team and their girlfriends will be there at two? I'll meet you there, O.K.?"

Lee didn't know what to say. Her pale face blushed and the blood swishing through her ears blurred her thinking. She hesitated and was embarrassed that she didn't have a quick, cute answer like the other girls. She finally managed to mumble an answer, "Can...can I tell you tomorrow?"

"Sure. Where is your next class? I'll walk with you there."

"Oh, I have to stop at my locker first. I'll make you late for your next class. You should go on."

"Don't worry about it. I have PE next." He smiled smugly, grunted and said, "Huh, the coach won't hammer me too hard if I'm late for his class."

"Okay, but my locker is over in the west wing of the building. "

"Let me carry your books," Jim said as he gathered up Lee's books with his jumbo hands. "Let's go."

Walking relieved some of Lee's nervousness, but things were still moving too fast. As they strolled together through the crowded hallway, other girls stopped, twisted their heads, and stared at what they thought an odd couple. They walked a long way without saying a word. It was awkward, and Lee felt she should say something, so she blurted out all at once, "Are you a good skater? I've never been skating before. You may want to take someone who can skate."

"I've watched you play basketball. You will do just fine. I'll teach you, if you go with me. Okay?"

"Okay. But I first have to ask my dad. I'll let you know tomorrow," she said while collecting her English book from the locker. "Just put my books in there." Jim quickly followed her order. "See you in Geometry tomorrow," Lee told him as she slammed the locker door and stepped away.

Jim stood infatuated, watching this shy, but gorgeous girl scurry down the hall to her next class. Lee's eyes filled with sparkles and a dreamy smile stayed on her face as she faded from his gaze.

———————

The skating party was a blast for Lee, but not what she had thought it would be. Donna had known Jim's parents and persuaded Ed to let Lee go to the skate party, agreeing to take her there and later go get her. Ed was working that Saturday, so he readily approved Donna's suggestion.

The guys skated only for a short time. As promised, Jim taught Lee how to skate. The two rolled along, hand-in-hand for a short while. Like most all athletic things, Lee was a quick study to this fast moving wheeled thrill. Soon the guys all separated from the girls and congregated at the pool tables. An unannounced, pre-planned pool tournament was to be played at the Easy Glider. Most of the girls migrated to the soda shop where they critiqued each others skating style and compared burn marks. Lee stayed on the roller rink, improving her newfound skill.

The guys gambled on the outcome of the pool games. Some clowned around, pushed and shoved each other, and took dares to do ridiculous things—things like spelling their names with perfectly articulated belches. The longest belch contest was won by Jim. The guy-things were all repulsive to the on-looking girls, and they mostly ignored them and stayed at the soda shop, chatting about their hair, the upcoming prom, and how they hated their stupid teachers. Lee stayed on the skating rink and continued to find her legs. Soon the party ended. Jim walked Lee to Donna's car and thanked her for coming to the party and told her, "I'll call you tonight if that's okay."

"Sure, what time?

"Oh, around seven. Is that okay? I have something to ask you."

Lee told Jim, "I had a fun time. Thanks for inviting me and teaching me how to skate."

"You bet. I'll talk with you a little later. Got to go now. The guys are waiting on me at the pool tables."

Donna's car pulled away.

Without asking, Lee told Donna, "I had a great time! Thank you for talking to Dad and getting him to let me go. I really do like skating."

"Skating? What about Jim? Do you like him?"

"Oh, he's nice, but a little inconsiderate. He left me on the skate rink to go play pool with the other guys. How could he do that?"

"Get used to it kiddo. That's just boys being boys. Hey, they don't change after they grow up either."

They both shared a laugh. It was the best day
Lee had had since moving from her mountains.

It was like a foggy mountain dream to Lee,
but different from anything she had ever seen. She
was going to the Prom with Jim. As promised, Jim
had called at seven to invite her. Without asking Ed,
Donna had approved the invitation. Ed would learn
later about the date. He would also learn that he was
obligated to get Lee the perfect evening gown and a
few other accessories for the Sibley High's annual gala
event.

Arm in arm, she, and Jim entered the highly
decorated gym, but she hardly recognized the place.
Where daily she ran drills and sweated at practicing
basketball, was an enchanted far away dance floor. Soft
sounds from a live orchestra wafted through the gym's
now paper mache skyline. Hanging from the ceiling
were large silver stars. Each glinted and twinkled,
reflecting light from candles placed on prom attendees'
tables.

On the wall, where her basketball team lined
up to do layup drills was a beautiful painting of a
golden rising moon. A river flowed from its base. A
showcased caption above read, "You are crossing it in

style. Welcome to Moon River Landing."

On reaching the golden moon, they were greeted by a pimple-faced sophomore wearing black rimmed glasses, a white sport coat, and a black bowtie. A red carnation matching the color of his ruddy complexion was pinned to his lapel. "Welcome to Moon River Landing. Please follow me," his breaking voice screeched.

Together the three entered the dancefloor/ basketball court. Several couples slow-danced there to the orchestra's ragged rendition of Henry Mancini's "Moon River." They were seated under the racked-up basketball goal located at the far end of court. The teen kid's cracking voice informed them as he lit the candles on their table, "You can help yourselves to refreshments. They are located at the end of the river... up there, where we came in." He pointed toward the gym's entrance. Then he lowered his arm, slid back his glasses on his nose, and swiftly marched away.

Lee was still bedazzled by the transformed gym. She peered about trying to identify things familiar and finding few. Jim watched her for a minute and then cleared his voice. He spoke loudly like he was calling a play on the football field. His voice rang out above the chatter and the orchestra, "Lee, would you like for me to get you some punch?"

On hearing his voice, Lee jumped as though awakened from a dream. She did not speak, but nodded.

The sophomore escort approached and directed another couple to their table. The seated young man was like Jim, a senior and was once on the football team with Jim. He had dropped out due to a slow healing cracked ankle his junior year. The young lady was not a senior. Lee remembered her from her freshman English class. She was a friend of the girl who had made fun of Lee when she first enrolled at Sibley. She wore a beautiful pink evening gown with matching long gloves. Her blond hair was coiffured in a tall beehive style. Oddly, she carried no purse, but instead strapped on her shoulder was a Polaroid Instamatic camera.

The now seated couples exchanged hellos.

"Hey, Ken," Jim shouted out over the background noise, "I was about to go get some punch for Lee. Would you care to go with me?"

Ken turned to his date, cupped his hand, and whispered in her ear, "Connie, would you like some punch. Jim and I are getting some."

"Why yes, I'd love something to drink," she voiced while nodding.

Jim and Ken left. Lee and Connie did not speak to each other and the tension was building. Lee, once again, began to scan the gym looking for familiar things from the basketball court. Connie rose, unstrapped the Polaroid, and walked away. She began taking pictures of other couples seated nearby. Soon returning with several readymade pictures in her hand, she laid them on the table beside the candles.

The familiar freshman English class friend saw Connie and made a beeline for her table. She was the girl who had made fun of Lee and referred to her as "Lo'rettie." Her name was Glenda.

Smiling and chomping fast on Dentyne chewing gum as she approached, her lips soon bunched up, and her eyes became fixed on the instant developed pictures that lay on the table. She wore a dress very similar to Connie's dress, but it was sky blue in color. Above her squatty forehead, her hair was styled identical to Connie's—a beehive.

"Oh hey there, Lo'rettie," she said while sneaking a reach for the stack of pictures. Boldly she then held them up close to her face, squinted, and as though insulted by what she saw, she asked, "*Who* is this in

this? It's too dark in here to tell who's in the picture!"
She drummed her fingers on the table.

Without waiting for an answer, a smirk twisted
up on her face and she angrily mumbled something.
With both hands she then extended the pictures near
to the candle's light. She bowed her body over the table
to get a closer look, her face coming dangerously close
to the candle's heat. Like a Sunday dinner yard-bird's
un-plucked feathers, her spray-coated hairdo began to
singe. The beehive glittered, faintly twinkling like a far
away star.

"What's that terrible odor," she snapped while
snarling and cutting her haughty eyes toward Lee.
Pointing at Glenda's head, Lee screamed at the top of
her voice, "Your hair is on fire! Your hair is on fire!
Stand still."

Quick as a cricket, Lee rose from her seat and
threw her wrap over Glenda's head, attempting to snuff
out the inflamed beehive. Glenda, in the dark to what
was going on, fought back, giving Lee a fierce shove.
She yanked the wrap from her head, flinging it to the
floor. A sporadic sparkle flickered from the smoldering
beehive. Panic now blazed from Glenda's face. Her eyes
looked like two full-moons and she became hysterical.
Frantically she patted her hair, unintentionally stoking

the embers. Desperately, she spun around and like a basketball player going for a long pass lay-up, she sprinted—toward the court's end, to the end of Moon River, and to the ladies' room.

Seeing the punch bowl, she made a split-second decision. She dunked her head in it. Soon a soaked head emerged, gasping for air. Her beehive now looked like a wet mangled crow's nest. Punch dripped and splashed on the floor as she crinkled her nose at yet another odd odor—the sharp smell of liquor permeating the air.

Jim, unbeknownst to anyone but Ken, had spiked the punch with a pint of Southern Comfort. Ken had distracted Mr. Gibson, the chaperon, by faking a need for help on a particular trigonometry problem. Ever eager to help, Mr. Gibson had taken the bait; he even led Ken to the far side of the gym where he showed Ken a use of the problem—an overhead triangular braced building truss.

Drenched, singed, and reeking of liquor-spiked punch, Glenda and her date left the prom early. Luckily, she was not injured. All other prom attendees enjoyed a lovely moonstruck evening at Moon River Landing.

Chapter 13 - COLORBLIND WINDS

Change was constant in Lee's junior year at Sibley High. She experienced it both on and off the basketball court. Like a clipper ship, she adjusted her sails and adapted to the prevailing winds of change. They transformed her character.

Lee was totally ignorant of black people but doubted the stories she'd heard about them while growing up in the mountains. For the first time in her life, now at Sibley she would attend a school with black students. In Fannin County, they represented less than one tenth of one percent of the population. Black families kept to themselves and lived in a shantytown located across the tracks on the backside of Blue Ridge. None had ever attended Fannin County schools. Those wanting to further their education were bused daily to Pickens County, a one hour trip each way. They congregated and studied in a schoolhouse with black students from several other North Central Georgia counties.

On the court, three circumstances changed that had a great impact on Lee's junior year:

1)   Girls' basketball became like boys' basketball.   Half court basketball went away and girls now ran the full court just like the boys.

2)   Black girls now practiced and a few even got to play in games.

3)   Lee had a new coach—her first ever female coach.

Lee's transition to full-court basketball was a snap.   She was fast on her feet and had always been able to outpace her opponent while dribbling. Because she was court-savvy and could pass the ball either bullet hard or biscuit soft, her new coach moved her to the point guard position.

She was short in height, but played with great desire and aggressiveness, a style she quickly learned from the black players. Among themselves they referred to her as "Honkie Go Girl" and later as just "G. G." With reckless abandon, she could bust a seam, race up the middle and score on opponents before they could turn around.   By midseason, through self-discipline and sheer hustle, Lee was the *de facto* court team captain.

With their winning season, Sibley was assured a playoff spot in the regional tournament that junior year. Maddox High, their last and pivotal season game, would determine their starting place in the playoffs. The Maddox game would again steer Lee's ship to another port.

———————

"I ain't doin' it. That chrome dome cracker, he be crazy if he think I gonna cripple Sister Golden Hair," said Ella, a tall, first-time-ever Maddox High black player. She muttered the words to another black team member seated beside her.

On bench edges the team sat facing each other in the Sibley gym locker room. In three minutes the start of the second half would begin. Maddox trailed Sibley by nine points in this crucial last game. The Maddox coach pondered the strategy he had chosen for reversing his team's losing position.

He wanted Sibley's team leader off the court and team sportsmanship did not matter. He also did not care who took her out. He simply wanted her gone from the game. Lee's presence was the only obstacle preventing his team from regaining the lead and advancing to the tournament. Based on experience, he was certain his victory plan would work.

"Ella," he shouted from near the locker room's only exit to the court. He spoke her name as though he'd just awakened from a bad dream. Fretfully he flicked his Lucky Strikes' ashes too hard, erringly flipping the cigarette from his fingers. Like a broken toy, it skipped and danced across the concrete floor. Hastily his shoe found it and stole its glow with a furious twist. His sly eyes looked up and he plucked at his lower lip as he walked toward Ella. He confidently fired his words, "You know what you have to do now, right? Every time number 12 brings that ball up the court, you full-court-press her hard and step on her foot, but not her pivot foot. Don't worry about the foul the ref might call on you. Got my meaning?"

Ella stared dejectedly at her ankle-high white-laced PF Flyer. She slowly turned her head, paused, and then raised it. Not making eye contact with him, she drew deeply from a well of decency and took a stand. Firmly she said, "No sir, coach. I don't be playing no nasty b-ball! I play straight ball. I ain't gonna hurt that girl like you say."

"Well, hell then girl! You just as well stay here in the locker room then! You want our team to lose, don't you? Don't you, now?" he screamed, hovering over her, glowering at her nappy hair with a look of disgust on his face. He flung up one arm and pointing toward the door and said, "Why don't you just go out there and join the rah-rah paper shaker girls?"

The coach pursed his lips, cocked back his head, and looked at the ceiling. All eyes watched him as he paced the locker room. He stopped, switched directions, and shouted to another black girl who had not played in a game all year, "What about you, Bernice? Do you want our team to win tonight? Are you afraid to step on toes to win the game?"

"No sir, coach," she said loudly as a crooked little grin formed on her plump blue lips. "I get dat girl gone and we win tonight. I don't be liking her none too much no way."

"That's what I like to hear. That's what I want to hear from all you girls. I want to hear you all say it. Say it with me: 'Win! Win! Win!'" The coach led them in a repetitive chant. The Maddox team left the locker room and promptly took to the court playing defense. Ella stayed behind, alone in the empty locker room.

Sibley took the ball out and it was quickly in Lee's hands. Like a water bug she weaved her way up court toward the goal. Bernice was trying hard to stay on her, but was falling behind.

Just as Lee was making a breakaway, she felt something awry. It was as though her feet weren't working; everything was happening but in slow-motion, and then all at once. Sensing loss of the ball, she grabbed for it while suspended in air. The ball stayed in bounds, but bounced into the hands of a Maddox player. As Lee crashed and slid on the hardwood floor, the Maddox player rushed with the ball to the opposite end of the court. There she put the ball on the glass for easy points, but points were not added to Maddox's score.

Lee lay motionless on the court at first, but five seconds later she managed to sit up. With her left hand, she steadied and held her right forearm. Agony flooded her face as she fought back tears. Lee's coach, Linda Kell, raced onto the court to Lee's side. The referee stopped the game. Coach Kell helped Lee slowly get up and walked with her on a painful slog to the Sibley bench. There, Donna, her step-mom, stood wringing her hands, beside Lee's team.

With flaming eyes, Coach Kell then spun around, ran to the referee, and confronted him. The Sibley crowd had already risen to their feet bellowing deafening boos. They wanted the right thing done.

The referee had clearly seen Bernice intentionally step on Lee's foot. He wisely deemed it a flagrant foul, called a technical and ejected Bernice from the game. Free throws were awarded to the Sibley team and all three were made, but afterward their game plan went adrift. Lee's team ran afoul, floated into a dead calm and sank into defeat.

When Donna delivered Lee to Grady Hospital she learned the fall on the court had caused Lee's forearm to be shattered. With a steel plate and screws, surgeons secured Lee's broken arm. She was also fitted with a support cast.

Without Lee's on-the-court leadership, Sibley was not the same team. From the sideline she cheered on her team in their first tournament game, but they still lost. Sibley's chance to play in the state tournament, and Lee's basketball career were over.

———————

Chapter 14 - GIRL CRUSH

The cast on Lee's broken wrist was going away. The diligent doctor's saw buzzed and cut. Fine white dust floated, filling the procedure room with a pungent odor. Prying and then gently removing the cast, he tossed it like a cracked egg into a trash bin. "Good riddance," Lee anxiously muttered, then gave him a sly relieved smile. He flashed back a smile, quickly examined her wrist, and removed the stitches.

The cast at first had brought her happiness; later torment and embarrassment. Since having the cast, each day at school Jim carried her books. Like a banner emblazoned with red, blue, and black characters, all her team mates and Jim's team mates had signed the cast. But after a month, the cast became a persistent pest—itchy, smelly and in the way, always in the way.

Her covered forearm and the scar where the incision was made to insert the titanium rod itched like crazy. No graceful, discreet way existed to lessen the torment. Lee fashioned a 'wrist scratcher' from a coat hanger. The scratcher, baking soda, and lots of will power made the itching and the odor tolerable.

Donna promptly drove Lee from the doctor's office back to Sibley High. In silence she stood by her locker briefly before going to class. There, like a fast dream just before waking, the incident took place, bursting forth and vanishing forever. Simultaneously someone touched her new scar and fondled her buttocks. Lee was startled and then enraged.

"Get your hands off me!" Lee jumped sideways, holding on to her high school locker door. Her English book, jammed with homework papers, tumbled to the tile. Creased inside, sheltered in the book, she had been reading Jim's note. She heard nothing, but then a transient scent—Listerine masking tobacco breath. Back turned to her, someone stood beside Lee. Turning, now face-to-face she was admonished:

"Be cool now dumplin. Don't be gettin yo drawers in a wad. I thought you be like me," the tall, high-yellow girl said. Easing back, she flagged palms on either side of her brown-sugar face. One cocked blue eye watched Lee.

She wore loose-fitting army fatigues suspended by a gray cord. Above a rear pocket flap she flaunted a sewn-on heart-shaped patch. Embroidered on the patch was "Kiss My Patch, Y'all."

The cocked blue eye saw Lee's dough-white face reddened, and was curious to her. Like a side-winder, the eye studied the splotches. Clues, gestures were sought—anything to redeem the mistake.

"Well, you thought wrong! I like boys! Get lost, creep!"

Goose bumps lined Lee's spine. Her eyes flitted. *Who had seen? What did blue-eyed black girl find?*

The scar—pink, sensitive, once cast secluded, but now exposed. Lee steamed ...

"Don't you *ever* touch me! You hear?" Nervous eyes continue scanning.

"Okay Golden Girl. We be cool! But, how was I to know? You always be looking at my blue eye. You all time be wearing pants like me, too."

"I ain't *nothing* like you. You stay away from me!"

Lee slammed her locker door, gathered, and tucked her homework papers back into her book. With her book under her arm, she turned and marched to her English class just minutes before the bell rang.

———

She hadn't recovered Jim's half-read note. She hadn't even seen it sail and settle under the wall-mounted heat radiator. Hidden and out of sight, like a limp-laced doily it rested there.

Her "touchy friend" *did* see it though. Hunkered down tying a loose boot string she glanced over and recognized it. Its sharp creases and flattened folds quickly identified it as not just another trivial school paper. Slightly intrigued and thinking never for a second that it was Lee's note, with one lean limb she made a slapdash grab. Up-righting her lanky frame, she cat-footed down the empty hallway. Creeping furtively along, she read the note. A conniving smile formed on her face when she read the last line:

"It's over. You're no good for me and I'm no good for you. So good-bye kiddo."

Bad news travels fast and it travels at the speed of light if the news is really bad. Lee had not seen Jim all morning, but she was picking up on some strange vibes in the hallways. Her classmates gave her only an okay hello when they passed by. Those she thought to be her friends did not initiate talk with her in class before the teacher began the lesson. Something was definitely up, but what?

Oh, Lord! Maybe someone saw her touching me. Maybe they think I'm that way too. But, where is Jim? Is he avoiding me? Why hasn't he met me at my locker between classes like he always does? Oh, well. I'll see him in the lunchroom if he's at school today.

———————

The clatter and chatter of the school lunchroom hummed in Lee's ears as she stood by a table holding a tray of food. Jim was seated with his rowdy gang— some boys from the football team. Not seeing Lee, one player seated one table over shook his fist and asked a player near Jim, "Hey, fart-face, you want a knuckle sandwich to go with that meat-loaf you're eating?" The other player curtly fired back, "Keep it up turd-head. Are you eating a banana or is that your nose? Come over here and I'll give you a fat lip!"

Today, no seat beside Jim was vacant and no player offered to move, allowing her to sit with Jim at lunchtime. She moved closer to Jim and said, "So, how's your morning going, Jim?"

He didn't look up. No one said anything, but instead they fumbled with their milk cartons, blew milk bubbles with their straws, or looked deep into their plates. Some glanced out the window, but none commented on Lee's missing cast, the one many of them had signed.

"Is something wrong, Jim? Why aren't you talking to me?" Lee spoke loud enough for people two tables over to hear.

Jim glanced up, but made no eye contact with Lee. Then he muttered, "Didn't you read the note I left in your locker?"

"Well, yes, some of ..." She shuddered. The incident passed through her mind and her pulse quickened. Words would not come.

"I'll save you some time. It's over. Me and you are through." Jim sprang from his chair, collected his tray items, and dashed toward the trashcan like he was sprinting for the goal line on a quarter-back sneak.

Lee, still speechless, stood in shock feebly holding a tilting tray. Her fork bounced from the floor as she watched him go, but she didn't see it. The lunchroom got quieter. Her plate crashed to the floor. All noise ceased, but the chatter soon returned. Nearby, eyes alternately focused on her and then Jim.

Suddenly all her questions were answered. Entering the cafeteria was a beautiful girl who looked taller and lovelier than the lady on a silver dollar. After offloading his plate and emptying his trash, Jim politely put away his tray. The skinny brunette girl locked arms with him. Together smiling at each other, Jim and the team captain of the rah-rah paper-shaker crew strolled away.

———————

A leper. A short blonde leper she was. Her classmates shunned her. Friendships became fragile and even her former basketball teammates kept their distance. She had a contagious incurable disease, but none openly or outwardly named it or acknowledged its existence. No treatment was available for being rejected by her school's most popular student.

Seeking comfort, she first denied it and buried herself in her studies. Poetry became a balm. She loved reading, especially poetry, but she was not inclined to write poetry—it required dealing with personal feelings. Something she'd rather leave stored away. Days dragged on.

In English class one day, the teacher informed the class, "Okay students, we have been studying the mechanics, the meter, and the meaning of poetry for about a week. Today, I want you to write and turn in a poem to me. It can be about anything. Anything you like will do just fine. Oh, and one last thing, it does not have to be a long poem. Four lines will do, but write more if you like. We may share them with the class later. You may begin now."

On this particular day, Lee was mildly depressed. She felt even writing her name would be a mountain too high to climb. Still, she gathered her thoughts and tried to fulfill the teacher's assignment. She scribbled down what she was thinking and feeling—her true feelings.

"Sometimes I often wonder, what's

the use in being alive.

When it seems everyone's against you

And nobody's on your side.

And once they spot this condition

the vultures begin to pound.

It seems they're really enjoying it,

hitting you while you're down."

Her poem was neatly folded, signed on the back, and turned in to the teacher. On the next Monday the graded poems were given back to each classmate.

Some poems were held by the teacher, who asked their authors to stand and read them to the class.

As the first poem was being read, Lee opened her folded poem and peaked inside at her grade. In bloody red ink she read, "F-" A note from the teacher was also inked beside the grade,

"Poetry is an uplifting art form meant to make others feel something positive. You can do much better than this. I expect you to at least try."

Lee's grades started a gradual slide after this point in her life, but she continued to read poetry. She stayed in her room, coming out only to join Donna and Ed at their evening meal.

Donna unsuccessfully encouraged Lee to get involved in some new sport, maybe softball, or maybe swimming.   Public pools were convenient.   That winter she tried to get Lee to join her bowling club. Lee showed no interest in bowling with the old folks, Donna's friends, and she told Donna, "I'd rather stay here and read in my room. Thanks for asking though."

Physical activity was not what Lee wanted. Being in control of her life was what she really wanted. She wished for one other thing: for everything to stop changing in her life. She dreamed of being back in the mountains where things stayed the same. Often she thought about just sitting on Granny's front porch, rocking in Granny's rocking chair and listening to the catbirds and the occasional mockingbird.

Her senior year, Lee was crushed. With no exercise and sneaking to eat, her body ballooned. Her pant size climbed. She wasn't really hungry when she ate, but eating somehow eased the pain and made her forget about what was making her sad.

Again, Donna tried to help Lee by limiting her food choices and portion sizes, but to no avail. When no one was at home she would take food from the pantry and hoard it in her room. Later, when melancholy came to call, she would gorge herself with the stashed treats.

Looking in the mirror one day, she was shocked and finally accepted reality. She was grossly overweight. Deep down, she already knew what the mirror had revealed. Her closet held clothes (and snack food), but those clothes would not fit her. On most days she wore extra large pants and a man's shirt. Lee reacted strongly, taking extreme measures to change the unwanted image.

Donna noticed the weight loss. She knew that Lee was eating well, but still she was losing weight. Even though Lee was a teenage girl, Donna sensed that Lee spent too much time in the bathroom. When questioned about the occasional vomit odor, in a resigned tone Lee would say, "Oh it's nothing. My stomach is just upset. That school food is gross."

Donna became uneasy and seriously concerned. To Lee's rancorous objections, she took her to see a doctor for a physical. The doctor gave her a clean bill of health and told Donna, "These weight gains and loss are quite normal for a developing young girl. It's just part of her becoming a woman. Lot of things are changing all at once in her body. There is nothing to worry about. She's just maturing."

Lee had matured faster than anyone knew since moving to the city. As a senior, her pant size shrank three sizes. She felt moderately good about the image she now saw looking back at her in the mirror, but her next battle would be a tough contender. Battling bulimia would be a tall feat and require all her best efforts.

Lee Ellen's coming of age was calamitous, but not

uncommon for many living in the Southern Appalachian Mountains. A social earthquake was taking place in the USA during the 1960s and the South was its epicenter. Its culture and way of life would never be the same. Its people responded by moving from the rural mountains to urban areas. There, they worked to make a better life for their families.

From the same Blue Ridge Mountain area of North Georgia, a young boy experienced his own wave of calamities fueled by the social earthquake. Many years later, the two would return to their roots—the Blue Ridge Mountains.

———————

THE
BOY

PART II

1953

"Children begin by loving their parents; as they grow older they judge them; sometimes they forgive them."

\- Oscar Wilde

Chapter 15 - THE FATTED CALF SWAP

My life set sail on Mill Creek, a place over near nowhere, but it wasn't the end of the world. Georgia, Tennessee, and North Carolina all converged near there and if you squinted hard on a clear day, you could see lots worse places to be than Mill Creek. In the 1950s, clear days there were scarce as hen's teeth because of air pollution.

That Tennessee Copper Company located across the state line and upwind from where I was raised was responsible for the pollution as it belched out "niter" and sulfur gases night and day. I, Jeff Cagle, of mostly sound mind and clear memory, recall seeing its vivid artwork. Like egg yolks splattered on blue canvas, that stinky stuff scribbled on the sky. When it drifted toward our farm—about three miles away—it caused our plow mules to cry. Mama cows, too, would tear up and hold milk from their babies. It choked and strangled everything green around it. Land nearby the smoke stacks looked like pictures of the moon—barren hill, gullies, red clay nothing. Luckily, our garden and corn fields got nipped a few times, but never killed.

The smell and taste I remember as well. Wet

smoldering stove wood gave off a similar odor. That sulfur in the air tasted like unripe persimmons and would pucker my lips. Breathing in and then swallowing made my stomach feel like I'd eaten too many green apples. My belly would be like two cats fighting inside a gunny-sack. Weeds somehow, especially Johnson grass, were never affected by the sulfur and acid rain. Skyward they grew alongside emerald stalks of corn.

Back then, hundreds of people lived in this tri-state area and life was good for them. They gladly worked for the copper mining company. Most folks reckoned the pollution a necessary evil and a reasonable compromise. It put food on their tables, a roof over their heads, and shoes on their children's feet. Most importantly, having a job with "The Company" meant they didn't have to work in the hot corn and hay fields, like my brothers and I did.

My entry to life was enabled and made good by a business deal between a notorious doctor and a horse trader. Dr. Hicks got a fat, white-face heifer calf out of the deal and my dad, the horse trader, got his seventh son delivered into the world. The deal was hammered out and agreed to at our farm, where Ole Doc Hicks made the house call.

Most would say Ole Doc got the better end of

that deal, but I strongly disagree. I feel lucky as a seven to have arrived alive and allowed to spend a little time with my parents, even though my time with each was precarious at best and always calamitous. Who snookered who on that fatted calf swap will be decided later, after I'm dead. Death tends to naturally sort out answers to life's hard questions. I can see my grand exit happening now.

On Mill Creek, the earthly remains of my spirit's temple will set sail for freedom. There, below the pristine waters of that little waterfall, my poured out ashes will swirl around and thrash about. Maybe a few will settle out on the green mossy banks of my youth. My lighter ashes—that glitzy and frothy residue that so often darted and dazzled and captured everyone's eye—will probably drift with the current on downstream. As lost as a feather in the wind, they will skim and stream through our cow pasture, on past that big flint rock where we farm boys sunned—our naked bodies clinging to its hot ragged face, after a chilling swim. They'll linger a while over the cool placid pool of the Ole Maple Hole where we'd seined for horny-heads, silver sides, hog suckers or maybe a lost spring lizard.

After a brief respite, onward my dust will sail, meandering through gentle wooded hills, laurel, and alder thickets, lush fields of fescue, and nodding daffodils. They'll merge with Fighting Town Creek, where Cherokees fought, immigrant miners and local farmers were baptized, and salamanders hiding under craggy cavernous banks watched all the meaningless subterfuge of foolish men. On farther downstream, like Huck Finn and Jim on their log raft, my carefree grit will continue its adventure. They'll slip on down and assimilate with the big water: the Ocoee, the Hiwassee, the Tennessee, the Mississippi, and finally, they'll ease on by the Big Easy. On to the Gulf they'll go, where my lighter stuff will set anchor for a while, waiting to be dispatched to the next port of call.

This is the story of a storm-tossed and almost shipwrecked life. That life set sail from Mill Creek, high in the Blue Ridge Mountains of Georgia.

———————

Chapter 16 - THE BIG D

I was five years old when it happened, but I remember it well. The day was just like any other hot August day in Georgia, when Mom, Dad, my older brother Jerry, and I entered that office. The town was Blue Ridge, Georgia, the county seat of Fannin County. We all were sweating profusely before we arrived at the top of the creaky old stairs that emptied into an entrance way to his office. Years later, I recall thinking those steps were like the stairs to Doc Adams' office on Gunsmoke.

I didn't want to be there. Chasing butterflies, rocking snakes, or just playing on the banks of Mill Creek would have been lots more fun. I couldn't imagine what would follow that day, but I sensed the outcome would not be good. Things like these a kid just seems to know. Things parents try to hide, kids somehow smell or taste them in the air.

We all stepped inside his dark moldy closet of an office. He stood up from behind a big paper-cluttered desk and announced, "Come on in folks. I've been waiting for you. This won't take long. Just need each of you to sign a few papers."

Jerry and I looked at each other. We knew he wasn't talking to us because neither of us could write yet. We all sat around a small table. Jerry and I tried hard to imagine where this was going. I started to ask him a question, but before I got one word out he pinched a frown and shook his head. That told me, "keep quiet little brother."

"Now Henry, I need you to sign here," which my dad did. Then he followed by saying, "Now, Ruby, I need you to do the same."

Mom didn't look at the paper she was supposed to sign. Instead she peered down at Jerry and me. Then she wept, muttering something like, "Henry, you know this isn't right for these boys."

Another fuss began. One just like all the many others Jerry and I had heard before. We knew the expected outcome. Someone—usually Mom— would storm out of the room, hurt and angry. But this time she didn't leave.

She quickly reached for the paper. With her other trembling hand, she wiped tears away and signed it. The Big D was on. I don't know what I lost that day. Maybe nothing, maybe a lot, but I'll never forget that day.

I say "nothing" because, even though legally divorced, Mom and Dad continued to live together. Each slept in a separate room at opposite ends of our farm house. It was a trapped arrangement from which she had no escape. Raising two children required money. She had no way to earn an honest income, and he refused to pay child support if she left.

"It's best for the sake of the children," they told each other and oddly, it *did* work. They argued less being *legally* divorced than they had being *legally* married, at least until Dad would get verbally or physically abusive. Then she would pack a few clothes and go stay with one of my grown siblings. Later, he'd apologize and she'd come home. The farm stayed afloat. The rushing rain-swollen waters of Mill Creek rolled on.

1958 - Late Summer

Chapter 17 - HOMER HERO

Like the plow mules we turned out to pasture at laying-by-time, Dad also kicked up his heels and ran free after the divorce. Unchained to the burden of marriage, he felt he deserved all the liberties of being a single man again. Married for thirty years, fathering nine children by Mom and currently living in the same house with her, would not deny him of his freedom. To Dad, the most important freedom was the right to see other women. He did this often and he cared not about the shame and hurt it caused, or what the community thought of it. When he left for the evening to see other women, Mom in anger sometimes told Jerry and me, "Your daddy's gone whore-hopping with one of them whores in town."

One such-labeled woman had a brother who worked on our farm. His name was Homer, and he lived rent-free alone in a little clapboard house out in our cow pasture. The house had no lights or indoor plumbing. Dad set up a running tab for Homer at the local grocery store, and he was paid by the hour. Mom gave him items from her garden and sold him milk, eggs, and butter, just as she did to all the folks of our small rural neighborhood. I wondered sometimes if

Homer, or Mom, knew that Dad and Homer's sister were seeing each other. If either did, they in no way let it show.

Homer was a thin, dark-skinned, wrinkle-faced little man. Around grownups, he was quiet-natured. His eyes were grey, but not like most grey eyes. Instead, they looked like faded denim—cold, too-still, and saying nothing. His eyes looked more lifeless than that dead calf we found frozen to the ground on that winter night down on Mill Creek.

Homer had a head full of solid white hair that he kept well groomed. He drenched it in Dixie Peach Pomade and every coarse strand was slicked straight back. He was reserved and confident, but had a haughty air about himself. At times he acted as though he was too good to be working on a farm. If not for all those furrows that lined his forehead, and if dressed in a suit, he would've resembled a Philadelphia lawyer, a senator or somebody important. But that forehead was a serious distraction with its rows. So deep, turnip greens would have grown in them, had seeds been planted in early spring.

Homer's teeth always fascinated me. The bottom teeth were long and twisted and one or two were missing. When thinking hard about something, while his cigarette simmered in his cupped palm, he hissed through those bottom teeth. The top teeth were even more astonishing. Each was wider than a kernel of hickory king corn. One was gold, but it didn't stand out too much because all his teeth were tobacco-yellowed. They were the same color as that stain between his two fingers, where he held his cigarette.

Downing longneck beers at the local beer joint and thumbing his nose at fate on Saturday night was Homer's favorite pastime, but he didn't limit that time to just Saturday nights. He was drunk as a skunk, head bowed, and hair hanging in his face, when my brother Frank and I saw him just before daylight one summer morning. We were coming home from a long night of catching chickens, a job I did from the age of eleven until seventeen. Homer was doing his dead level best to stay astride a spooked mule—not his mule, but one he'd taken from our barn and saddled with a split-bottom army saddle. He had ridden the mule to town to imbibe a bit at Ralph and Grady's Beer Joint.

As Frank turned on a blind curve of The Old Epworth Road, the headlights of our panel truck placed the mule and Homer squarely on stage in the spotlight that morning. Startled, the mule jumped and skittered sideways. Homer didn't look up. Instead, both his hands held tightly to the saddle. We didn't stop to chat, but drove on home.

Later in the morning, when Mom went to milk the cows, she discovered the mule. Swishing its tail and stamping a front foot, but still saddled, he stood grazing the dew-covered fescue that lined the trail around the barn. Without any help or directions from Homer, the mule had delivered him safely to the barnyard gate, but Homer was nowhere in sight.

Mom removed the saddle, unbridled the mule, and put him back in his stable. Later she asked Jerry if he knew anything about the mystery mule, all saddled up with no rider or no place to go. He did not.

———————

Jerry and I didn't see much of Homer for the rest of that summer. Mom had put two and two together and told Dad about the mule and Homer's drinking problem. The rest of the summer, Homer stayed mostly out of sight. From our hilltop house, we could see him at a distance, working down in the meadow beside different parts of Mill Creek. He would be swinging an axe. Dad had told Homer to clear all the alder bushes from both sides of Mill Creek.

After Indian summer, and before the leaves started to change their color, Jerry and I—quite by accident—were once helped by Homer with a common farm chore. A half Jersey, half Angus, blue-nose cow had freshened with a new baby calf. It was a Saturday, about dark-thirty time. Dad had already showered, dressed, and left the farm for his date, but he had given Jerry and me a chore. "You boys go out in the woods and the pasture. Find that freshened cow and her new calf. Put them in a clean stable and give her two scoops of cottonseed meal. In the morning, give her two more scoops and milk her. Now y'all be careful. Sometimes a new momma acts crazy after she's just had a baby, especially them that's got some Angus in them."

Dad was never shy about giving Jerry and me hard things to do. Most all were more than I could do alone, but Jerry, being older and bigger than me, could usually handle whatever Dad gave us to do. But this job turned out to be far more than either of us could safely handle.

We found the cow and her newly born calf near a horse-apple tree, the one close by the house where Homer lived. Fallen apples from that tree looked rough, but were really tasty after the yellow jackets were shooed away. Grey, rusty marks coated these greenish-yellow apples, but Mom could make great fritters and jam with them. Sometimes she'd save away a few in our root cellar near the tater bin.

A drizzle of rain had fallen all afternoon and the ground surrounding the apple tree was soft and soggy—a really red, muddy mess. Walking in the pasture that evening was slippery. The cow and her calf did not take cover underneath the apple tree. Oddly, they stood over beyond the edge of the tree's shelter from the rain, out in the fog and drizzle. Jerry and I took cover under the apple tree, and studied a plan for getting the cow and calf to the barn.

To Dad's credit, he had advised us well. The new momma cow acted disturbed and ill as a hornet, and she paced around in circles. She was small and colored black and tan like a jersey, but she wasn't a pure bred. With her head tilted down she'd lunge forth as though she was butting a shadow attacker. She also bawled short, quick bellows, like a momma cow does when she's calling to her lost calf. But her newborn stood right there beside her. She was nervous and agitated, but she didn't appear to know why. Jerry and I stood and watched her in bewilderment, as globs of rain fell and splattered under the apple tree. We were both scared to go near this crazy cow.

The drizzle had stopped when we heard Homer close the door of his house. He looked like he was in his Sunday-go-to-meeting Church clothes, but he wasn't.

He wore a dazzling white shirt, clean khaki pants, and white socks inside his penny loafers. He swaggered toward us with the confidence of a Holiness preacher approaching a podium, but didn't join us under the apple tree. Even at a distance I could smell the fragrance of his abundantly applied Old Spice cologne. Then with arrogance in his big, boss-man bass voice, he demanded, "What'er you boys trying to do?"

Jerry sheepishly looked up and hesitantly responded, "Well..., uh, we're supposed to get this cow and her baby into the barn, but she's not acting right. I'm sort afear'd to bother her until she settles down some."

Homer gave a smug snicker, smirking confidently at our youthful lack of nerve. Then he began a speech, one that became a class on how to deal with cows. "A cow—'specially a cow that has just come in with a calf—acts funny and ya gotta watch 'em close. But now, the 'mainest thang' is, ye never let 'em know you're afear'd' of 'em. 'Ya gotta show 'em who's boss."

He then paused and removed an almost fresh pack of Camel cigarettes from his shirt pocket. Gazing at the cow, he pecked the pack against his index finger, grabbed one from the pack, and stuck it between his dry cracked lips. Quicker than a hummingbird, he clicked his lighter, took a deep drag on his Camel, and continued his teaching. "Boys, you don't know it, but when I lived in Florida, I worked on a thousand-head dairy farm. I was all the time axed to take kear of problems like this. Ya see boys...I ain't skeerda nuthin'. There's really not much to it. Y'all stand back there and watch, and I'll show you how it's done. Next time, y'all won't be so skeerd and'll know how to do it."

Homer took another long drag on his smoke, then rocket-fast he flipped it. Landing in the soaked red clay, it sizzled and smoldered. He looked straight at the momma cow and with almost humbleness in his voice, Homer informed her, "Sah now, heifer. Me and you is going to the barn."

Strangely the cow quickly bobbed her head toward the ground, almost as though she understood and was in agreement with Homer's words. Then like a warrior going into battle, Homer charged the cow.

Reading his sudden approach, the cow did not hesitate. She burst into a gallop toward Homer. With head bowed almost to the wet ground she scooped and lifted the little man off his feet. A half second later, Homer found himself draped over the cow's head, lying on his belly facing opposite her charging path. He fiercely hugged her neck as she sprinted down the muddy hillside. It all looked as wrong as sin on Sunday, but Jerry and I didn't know what to do.

Then, quick as a flash that cow stopped, sending Homer flying through the air, then crashing to the soggy soil, where he tumbled and rolled. Seeing Homer lying stunned and mired in the mud, the bodacious bovine sprinted back for another sortie. She lowered her head again and used it to root and roll Homer along the soggy soil, moving him farther down the hillside and closer to Mill Creek. She proceeded to grind Homer's glowing white shirt—with more of Homer now found outside the shirt than inside it—into the rain-soaked red Georgia clay.

Sufficiently satisfied with her work, the mad momma froze in place, looked wild-eyed mean down toward the creek, and gave a faint moo. With swollen udder and tits flopping from side to side, she hurried back to the side of her baby calf. There she held out and kinked her tail and let out short repeated bellows. She seemed now to be studying whether to stay by her baby's side or to go give Homer another butt, ride, and roll in the mud.

Before she could decide what next to do, Homer, looking more like mud than man, stumbled to his feet, limped at first, but then trotted fast toward refuge. Not looking back, he splashed a trail in the wet grass to his safe abode—back to the little house in our cow pasture.

Jerry and I stayed in the shelter of the apple tree a while longer and watched a proud momma lick and groom and bond with her calf. Later, when the calf had started to suckle from its mom, we sneaked away. We had failed to complete Dad's order but, as kids, we didn't want to pay the steep price Homer paid for his vanity that day.

That's the last time I saw Homer. He moved from that little house on Mill Creek. Maybe it was coincidental, but my dad stopped seeing his sister a short time after Homer's run-in with the mad momma cow.

————————

Chapter 18 - OUT IN THE WOODS

The last leaves on the trees were gone. Leafless trees signaled hog killing time on our farm. Hogs were normally killed and dressed at the top of a hill above our house, but today it was a calf. Climbing to the top was tiring, but once there, you could see things. You could look down on tree tops, see critters and other things scurrying out in the woods.

This day little stirred. At first, all Jerry and I saw were spindly pines and barren limbs swaying under a hanging gray sky. About a quarter mile away we saw Ole Vic King. He was out swinging an axe, cutting firewood, but we couldn't hear the crack of the wood chopping. The restless wind whistled loud and cut right through our thin-threaded Wranglers.

Ole Vic's tarpapered shack was down the hill and up a holler from us. It rested on the banks of a spring branch. A blue haze swelled up and curved away from its chimney, then floated down the holler. The branch trickled through the woods for about a half mile, then crossed the Old Epworth Road and then on to Mill Creek.

Dad had warned both Jerry and me on many

occasions, "Ole Vic's a lunatic. You boys don't go near him and stay away from his place out there in the woods." Mom too, had told us, "Ole Vic ain't right in the head, boys. Better y'all stay off his property."

I'd only seen Ole Vic up close once in my life. He looked all washed out. His face was clean shaved but it was whiter than the inside of a flour sack. His long scraggly hair looked like a comb hadn't been through it since he was a kid. He smelled like stove wood, and as he passed by that day, he didn't look up or say a word. He just eased on down the porch steps of Mr. Newman's Grocery. His big, thick fingers held high and close to his chest a brown paper bag full of store-bought groceries.

Getting that calf to the top wasn't easy. Jerry, the calf, and I started our march up the hill right after dinner. My brother was in the lead, holding the end of a calf rope. On the other end was the calf, and finally me behind this yearling. My job was to swat the calf on the hind legs with a hickory switch when she balked, which she did repeatedly.

We took a jagged path because the calf was cantankerous and refused to go straight. She'd stop in her tracks, look back at me with those curly heavily-lashed, innocent eyes, and nervously twitch her tail. Then, all of a sudden she'd hunker up and relieve herself. Then she'd jerk her head and dart out, running like yellow jackets were after her. Into the briers and the underbrush she dragged Jerry. I wondered if she didn't somehow suspect her fate.

She was the same calf whose momma had upended Homer and mired him in the mud several months back. She had grown fast, but she wasn't tame, and had never been haltered or led anywhere before this day.

Jerry liked the calf. When he fed her, he'd take a clean, hardened corncob and curry her thick black-and-tan winter coat. He also made sure her stable was extra clean. Weekly, if it wasn't raining, he'd go out in the woods to gather and carry fresh leaves to bed her stable.

We finally got the calf to the top, where Jerry tied her to a maple sapling. He told me, "You stay here and mind her. I'll be back in a few minutes." He trotted back down the hill.

In less time than it took to shuck a bushel of corn, he returned rolling a wheelbarrow. In it were an eight pound sledge hammer, and two sharp skinning knives. In its bottom was at least a gallon of crushed corn.

He removed the sledge hammer and knives.

Then he rolled the wheelbarrow over to where the calf was tied, and parked it right under her nose. She immediately started eating. Jerry asserted, "Prisoners get a last meal before they die, so you should too." He watched her eat. Sorrow smothered his face. Then, as though awakening from a bad dream, he shouted into the wind, "I'm going to get her a bucket of water." And he did.

After eating and drinking, that calf didn't move a muscle. She stared out into the woods, almost as if she sensed something out there that we didn't.

Then we got a surprise—Mom showed up. She'd come to see how we were doing. Looking somewhat ill at Jerry, she demanded, "What have you boys been doing? Why don't y'all have this little ole calf skinned by now?" She looked out into the woods, toward Ole Vic King's place, shook her head, and pretended disappointment. Then she mildly scolded Jerry, "I'll swan boy! I thought you could get this job done."

With tears welling up in his eyes, Jerry turned and trotted away toward the edge of the woods. Mom and I couldn't see his face, but I knew he was crying, because his shoulders were jerking up and down. As the wind whistled louder through the tree branches, he suddenly turned and faced Mom. "I can't kill this calf! I just can't do it," he screamed. This calf is... is my friend, Mom." Jerry bolted into the woods, sobbing as he fled.

Mom stood like a statue. Her face said nothing. Then a flood of emotions streamed across her face, and she reached for the sledge hammer. Three seconds later, the calf lay lifeless on the ground. She'd slammed the calf between the eyes. Then she gave me an order. "Jeff, untie that calf and hand me a knife." I jumped to it and did as she asked. Seconds later, steam from the calf's blood drifted upward. Blood trickled down the hill. Frosted oak and yellow poplar leafs were coated crimson. It pooled in shallow trenches.

Ten minutes later the calf's head and hide lay on the ground. She filled the wheelbarrow with them. Starting to roll it down the hill, she made a sudden stop. Placing her hands on her hips she turned and ordered, "Jeff, go to the barn and get a shovel. Come back and dig a deep hole out yonder in the woods. Then bury this offal in it. Mind you, stay on *our* property. Don't you go near Ole Vic King's place."

I began my work. Like a veteran warrior she marched from the hilltop. Near sunset the wind died down. As I finished burying the calf's remains, I could now hear it—the crack of wood being chopped out in the woods.

————————

Chapter 19 - SHOES

The storm clouds had been gathering for a long time. Mom and Dad were not getting along in their new arrangement—divorced but living together. The arguments raged and got worse between them. The verbal abuse had turned physical. I learned that the true toll on the road of compromise is high.

At this same time of my life I learned my identity. By identity, I mean where people like me fit into the overall American socio-economic system. For the first time I saw, felt, and cried uncontrollably about my status. I had never even asked the question, who am I, but I learned that I belonged to a particular class—a group of people having many common attributes: The Working Poor. They worked and they were poor. Today, we would be called "white trash" or "rednecks" or maybe even "trailer trash," except back then, no one lived in mobile homes.

No longer able to tolerate Dad's middle age crazies, Mom moved us to the big city—Chattanooga, Tennessee. Mom, Jerry, and I left Dad and the farm down on Mill Creek. Don, Nace, and Frank, my next older brothers had already left the farm and now lived with one of my two sisters, Peggy Sue Watkins. Mom's move was precipitated by one of a string of domestic quarrels about nothing, as far as my young childish mind could discern.

We lived in a two room flat that shared a bathroom with four other families in a big mansion-like house. Definitely it was bigger than any house I'd ever seen back home. One room was the kitchen. The other was the living room and it had a bed in it. We all three slept together in that one bed.

The big house, located at the base of Missionary Ridge, was not what it seemed at first glance. From the curb, the stairways, the front porch, and the cornices were ornate and it flaunted wealth. A close up look, however, revealed an old dilapidated house badly in need of paint and repairs, and the yard was tiny. The big house setting on that little lot reminded me of what a regular horse saddle on a Shetland pony looked like. Jerry and I were used to roaming acres of fields and woods down on Mill Creek. The yard with its little fish pond was nice, but nothing compared to the Maple Hole down on Mill Creek where we'd dam up, swim jay-bird naked, and seine for fish with a burlap feed sack.

Jerry and I attended a school where the students were from another particular class of people—children of the working affluent. They were city folks. The really rich kids didn't go there. They went to private schools like McCallie and Baylor. The students I went to school with were clean, well groomed, and wore nice clothes—they never wore the same clothes two days in a row. They always had allowance money to buy snacks. They reminded me of that kid I'd seen on TV named Beaver Cleaver. Most weren't friendly to me. Most would not even talk to me.

I sat in the back of the class beside a kid who would talk to me. He dressed like all the other kids, but he was kind of stupid. One day he bet another kid his snack money that he would eat glue. And he did and he won the bet.

Most of those kids acted as though I stank, but I didn't stink. Every day my Mom made me strip naked and wash at the kitchen sink. Those kids didn't like me because I wasn't dressed like them. The boys wore plaid shirts and penny loafers with real pennies in them. My clothes were much different. Mom made my shirts. My jeans were Jerry's hand-me-down Wranglers, bought new the previous fall from Jabley's, located in McCaysville, Georgia. When we lived down on Mill Creek if she had money—usually saved from selling milk and eggs—Jerry and I would get a new pair. Mom took none of her trade to another clothes merchant. She'd once witnessed there a moral indiscretion between a strapped-for-cash shopper and the shop owner. At all times, my other pair of jeans lived on pants stretchers, hung up to dry inside the apartment. Mom didn't tolerate her boys going round nasty. "It's no shame being poor, but it is a shame being nasty," Mom told Jerry and me.

The day I learned my place in the socio-economic spectrum, we were playing two-hand touch football on that tiny lawn with the fish pond. A small dog first watched the game from under the porch, but then he decided to come and be a part of it. He would chase one of us and then another. He didn't care who carried the ball, but seemed more interested in the shoes the players wore. He would try to bite at the heels of the fleeing player.

My shoes were not in good shape. To avoid the expense of buying me a new pair, Mom had stitched them together once with a needle and brown thread. "Making do" was what Mom called it. They held together, but later the thread hung loose from the heel. The thread intrigued the dog. He chased me, nipping at that dangling brown thread, and finally chomped down on my heel, ripping the shoe from my foot. The shoe lay on the small, green lawn for about two seconds. I turned, saw it, and ran to save it. The dog ran to the shoe and beat me to it. He picked it up with his teeth, then tore away down the street holding high his trophy aloft—one of my only two shoes.

The other kids weren't concerned about the theft of my shoe. In that moment of fun, they just laughed at me as they pointed at the fleeing dog. They didn't know that shoe was one of the only two shoes I had. Those shoes were supposed to last me until Christmas when maybe I'd get a new pair. As a child, Christmas meant getting new clothes and not toys like the wealthy kids.

I didn't chase the dog to get my shoe, but I should have. Jerry looked at me with questions written on his face, but said nothing to embarrass me. Once again, Mom would have stitched it up because she had no extra money to buy new shoes. Once again I would have had to MAKE DO. I've never felt as poor and as burdensome to Mom as I did on that chilly fall day when I had to tell her a dog had stolen my shoe. That's the day I learned the meaning of poverty in America.

My Mom worked hard every day. In Chattanooga she rode the city bus to work. She had no skills that paid good wages. The parents of the kids I went to school with were just the opposite. Mom worked at a curb-service drive-in, where she wore a white dress, an apron, and a white crown-like hat. She scooped ice cream treats. Mom also took in some ironing to help pay the rent, and to feed two hungry boys. My dad refused to pay any child support. I often wished we were living back on Mill Creek where I had never known we were poor.

———————

Chapter 20 - THE CHRISTMAS CHARADE

Christmas was a lie, as phony as Clara Belle the Clown and those other characters on TV. It was more fake than those plastic poinsettias Mom kept by the kitchen window, and would sometimes mistakenly water. Even before my first day of school, I knew Santa was not for real. Down on Mill Creek the fat man never once came to our house. He didn't stop at my best buddy Ben Thompson's house, either. He *did* stop at my friends Shirley and Tommy Harper's house, but he left them no toys. Like me, they didn't think he was for real either, but their younger siblings did, so Santa left only them toys.

Christmas was going to be different this year. Different in ways I had never dreamed. It would be the first Christmas I'd ever experienced in a big city. Even with my new Chattanooga address, my thoughts about Santa were unchanged—I didn't think he was for real. This year, again, I expected to get no toys. Still, kids talking at school about what Santa would bring them caused me to think again about my doubt. Their talk made me think that maybe I'd been wrong. It gave me some encouragement and hope against all hope that toys would somehow arrive at our small apartment.

Maybe naughty or nice meant something different in the city. Maybe city kids had a different Santa from the Santa who always failed to visit kids down on Mill Creek. Maybe I had been wrong about a lot of things.

This Christmas season began as the best ever, but later turned out to be the worst ever—Christmas holidays never to be forgotten. Jerry and I weren't able to get jobs to make any Christmas money. The *Chattanooga Times* didn't need us to deliver their newspapers. Selling the *Grit* in Chattanooga also wasn't possible. With only Mom working, money was tight as bark on a black oak tree and Christmas was only a few days away. Still, Jerry and I remained hopeful.

My sister Evelyn and her husband Roy lived in Chattanooga, where they both had good jobs—Roy worked for Southern Bell Telephone and Evelyn was a cosmetologist. They had a blue, two-tone car—a 1955 Bel Air Chevy. During the Christmas holidays, they were driving it to McCaysville to visit with our other siblings. Mom, Jerry, and I were invited to go with them. It would be our first visit back home since we had left Dad on the farm to move to Chattanooga. This holiday trip changed my life. My outlook on Christmas would never be the same, as a result.

I don't know how my dad knew we were visiting.

News in a small rural community just seems to spread faster than fire in a sage grass field on a windy day. Dad got the news and acted quickly. He wanted us all back on the farm, and he wasted no time in making contact with Mom to make his plea. He wanted her to come back home to Mill Creek.

Jerry and I were not included in the bartering that went on between our parents. We stayed at our brother Bill's house while Mom and Dad went out to eat at a place on the Blue Ridge Highway called The Sanoga Café. This was the first time I recall them ever going out to eat together. As farm folks, we didn't do things like eat in a café. When we lived on the farm, we grew all our food and Mom cooked it for us on a wood stove. The blue speckled electric range was rarely used—the range whose enamel had been chipped by heat from the wood stove. Dad insisted that his meals all be cooked on the wood stove. He told anyone who would listen, "Stuff cooked on a wood stove just tastes better."

When Mom and Dad returned from the café, Jerry and I received some great news. Not that Mom and Dad were getting back together—Mom hadn't yet made her decision about moving back to the farm.

Instead, Dad told Jerry and me that we were

going to get toys for Christmas this year.

We would each get twenty dollars worth of toys from Williamson's 5 & 10 Store in downtown McCaysville. Dad told us a charge account had already been set up for us there. We could buy whatever we wanted as long as we didn't go over twenty dollars. Jerry and I could hardly wait to go pick out our toys— toys Santa had never given us at Christmas.

Williamson's 5 & 10 was better than being at Santa's Workshop itself. They had a big toy department and it had more toys than I had ever imagined Santa having at the North Pole. Rows of toys were stacked to the ceiling.

Before going into the store, Jerry and I had written down our toy wish list on the back of a brown paper bag. But when we got inside and saw all the toys, we both forgot about the list. We changed our minds several times about what toys we'd take home.

At the top of Jerry's list was an electric football game, complete with members of two opposing teams. The game was started and controlled by an electric switch knob that made the lined green football field vibrate. When switched on, the opposing players would move in all directions and sometimes they even moved the wrong way. We had both seen the toy football game on TV.

At the top of my wish list was a pair of Gene Autry six-shooters and matching holsters. Also, I got a cowboy hat to go with it. In the store I strapped them on. Strolling through the high canyons of stacked high toys I would stop and practice my draw. I had wanted a B B gun, but it cost too much, so I settled for the six-shooters instead, along with a few other toys I'd seen on TV.

Williamson's also had a candy department. We agreed to buy Mom some candy. A glass showcase displayed all kinds and flavors—hard peppermint sticks to soft chewy chocolates. Fudge, both chocolate and peanut butter varieties, was there. Jerry and I bought Mom fifty cents worth of each type of fudge. We also bought ourselves some candy, and ate it as we browsed the long rows of toys. Deciding what toys we wanted was not easy because we had never purchased any store-bought toys.

When the lady at the cash register totaled up my selected toys, she told me I had about a dollar left on my account. Quickly I went back to the toy department and picked up another toy—a giant spinning top made of thin metal, with a red wooden handle at the end of a spindle. Painted on the toy's tapered surface were clowns riding horses on a carrousel. As the top would spin, the horses galloped along. Up and down and round and round the clowns would ride as it rotated.

Jerry too, had money left over on his account, but he didn't get more toys. He asked for and got money back from the check-out lady at Williamson's.

We didn't get to play much with those gifts during the holidays, but seeing them made Mom happy—the happiest I'd seen her in a long time. She was almost as giddy as Jerry and I with our new toys.

She and Dad drove from McCaysville back to Chattanooga to our apartment. They picked up our sparse things and took them back to the farm on Mill Creek. Jerry and I stayed and played with the toys at Bill's house until the move was finished.

When we returned to the farm, we started right back where we had left off before our move to the city. Morning and after school chores were done seven days a week. Wood was chopped for both the wood cook stove and the Warm Morning heating stove. Other chores, like repairing the ever-collapsing farm fences, were always given to Jerry and me, especially on Saturdays. Clearing trees from a new ground with an axe to make room for more corn to be planted was also a hard chore.

It was the second Saturday after Christmas when I knew Christmas was over for me as a kid. That morning with my holstered six-shooters strapped at my side, I sat on the floor watching Roy Rogers on our black and white Philco TV. At the same time I was pumping the spindle to set my big top spinning. I released and watched the clowns go around and around on the carousel. Then Dad entered the room.

Something about the spinning top set off his Scots-Irish temper. He became enraged and rushed toward the top, which he dropkicked. Crashing and bouncing off the walls, it continued to spin and scurry about. It slid and spun erratically across the linoleum floor, finally coming to rest, wedged under the Warm Morning stove. He pointed his finger at me and bellowed, "Those people there on that TV aren't real. They're like all them toys you keep playing with. They're phonies. You need to stop watching that TV. Now get out of the house! Go to the barn and shuck corn and rearrange the hay in the hayloft or organize the plows and horse collars in the tack room. We ain't got time to be playing with toys here on the farm. There's plenty work needs doing. Now get out of the house and get to work!"

I grabbed up the dented top and raced out the door.   Jerry was already in the barn working.   We decided to bury our toys out there under the hay loft. Days when rain pelted the barn's tin roof, we'd sneak them out from hiding and unbeknownst to Dad, we'd secretly play with them in the hayloft.   Those hidden toys were the first and last Christmas toys I ever received from my Dad.

———

1965 - Autumn

Chapter 21 - LOVE LEAVES HOME

One at a time, we all eventually fled the farm down on Mill Creek. My older brothers and sisters were first to go. They grew up, got married, went to college, started a business, or got a job and moved into town. Dad held on until the bitter end. He sold the farm, married again, and returned to his familiar refuge in Akron, Ohio where, as a young man he and his siblings had fled when the Great Depression ended. Jerry was next to flee the farm.

———

At the supper table Jerry and Dad had a man-to-man discussion. The topic was about Jerry leaving the farm. He would go to live with Bill's family, and would sleep in a small bedroom in the office of the Cagle Poultry Company, a small company owned by my oldest brothers, Bill and Max. He would earn money by working on the weekends helping Max service the chicken trucks. The details had all been worked out, and Mom and Jerry had talked it over in private, before Dad came home that evening.

Jerry was the boss on the farm. He worked faithfully and could do just about anything that needed doing around the place. But now he had some dreams of his own he wanted to pursue. Like our older brother, Don, Jerry hankered to play football. Don was a former captain of the football team, and football scholarship player at Tennessee Tech, and Jerry could see himself following in Don's footsteps. His leaving home was to be expected though, because most all the Cagle boys left home early. Some left even before they graduated from high school. Frank, Nace, and Don had all left to live with our sister Peggy and her husband, Walter. Jerry wanted Dad's permission to follow his dream, but Dad's acceptance was what he really wanted. Dad's permission was nice, but not necessary. That's how Jerry really felt about it.

I didn't want Jerry to leave and, as the white horse slowly marched us down the hillside closer to Mill Creek, I told him so. I felt that he was abandoning me. I wanted him to be happy, but if Jerry left, all the farm work would become my responsibility. *Was I ready for this big change?* I asked myself.

But it was more than that. I wouldn't have anyone to talk to anymore. If Jerry moved away, who would answer my questions? Those important boy questions... like who would win in a fight between Roy Rogers and Gene Autry? Is country music *really* here to stay? More recently I had questions of another nature, like why do girls look funny when they run? And why did we have so many brothers and so few sisters in our family? Also, I thought that he would no longer be my brother if he moved away.

At school, he would be just another older kid and, maybe, he would act like that little adopted girl at school, the one that always ignored me when people whispered she was my bastard half-sister. She heard the whispers too. We looked at each other, but we never talked to each other. Looking without talking was a personal problem I had and would cause me many problems later in life.

In my class at school, I was small. If Jerry left, maybe he'd no longer protect me from the older bullies at school. Maybe. But mostly, I feared that Mom and Dad would be disappointed in me when they saw that I wasn't able to do all the things that Jerry did on the farm. I felt small and alone, and thought Jerry's decision was selfish.

It was strange that I didn't want him to go. Truth is, we constantly fussed, argued and fought. Usually it was about nothing. We sharpened each other's mettle, and our behavior was normal and to be expected between brothers, some might argue. Well, maybe they were right, but I felt we were total opposites—like salt and pepper or oil and water. I also felt that Jerry, with his blond hair and great All-American Boy looks, was Mom's fair-haired child. I was just the runt baby of the family, and I had always felt this way.

Jerry and I had totally different personalities and now Jerry was becoming different in another way. He was becoming a man while I was still a kid. Jerry wanted to make his own decisions, and he did. He moved away. I wanted to slug him for leaving me, but I also wanted to hug him. Confused and sad, I also wanted to cry about my situation, but I didn't. Crying wasn't allowed. That's what my rowdy chicken catcher buddies told me. They were my new friends and work buddies. They worked for Cagle Poultry Company and sometimes I worked with them since I was getting older. I wanted to be like them.

After Jerry left, my workload on the farm went up, and I didn't get to make much money catching chickens. Dad really needed my help. Driving the farm truck and hauling farm animals was great fun, too, but I missed a lot of school to help Dad.

———

Epworth School is where I saw her for the first time. She had been moved over to another desk in my eighth grade classroom. Now she sat across from me. The teacher moved her there, away from a group of girls who previously had sat together, talking during class, and disturbing the teacher.

"Hey! What happened to your arms," she blurted out pointing her finger at me. "You look like someone threw you in the briar patch. Where'd you get all those bloody scratches on your arms?"

I was immediately embarrassed. Fearing to talk to a girl, especially a girl as beautiful as her, I stared at the top of my school desk with eyes wide open. Reaching on the desk's underside, I fidgeted with a wad of bubble gum stuck there.

She had the bluest eyes and her hair was the color of sourwood honey.   She crinkled her brow, pinched her lips, and stole quizzical glances at me— first at my red-festered chicken scratches, then at my tucked-down face that was glowing cherry red. Intrigued by my shyness, she poked me in the ribs with her school-bus-yellow pencil, and persisted with questions, "Okay, Jeff. Jeff is your name isn't it? What happened to you? Tell me."

I sheepishly raised my head and peeked at her once, then looked straight ahead at the chalkboard.

With one hand she covered her mouth, muffling and hiding a snicker. Her head remained turned toward me and she glowered at my big crimson ears. A grin stayed on her face.

"Yeah, that's me" I said, pulling a black bandana big as a flour sack from my back pocket. My hands shook like a mule in summer fly-time, as I wiped sweat from my face and palms. That's all was said. I didn't try to explain that I caught chickens at night, and that chickens had scratched my arms. Also, I didn't brag and tell her that I made good money catching chickens—two dollars a night and sometimes more. I figured she wouldn't understand such things anyway.

Our teacher rose from behind her desk. Towering close to six feet tall, Mrs. Abernathy took three long strides toward the chalkboard, spun around, and sternly told the class, "Okay, get quiet. Today you will learn how to diagram sentences. You need to listen carefully to what I'm going to say." The room became a graveyard.

Her name was Lee Ellen Bandy and she sat one row over from me in the eighth grade—my second try at the eighth grade. I failed my first try because Dad kept me out of school to work on the farm. She spoke to me first, because I didn't usually talk to girls. I was super shy and had never been around girls very much.   My sisters were already grown and married when I entered school.   Some girls near my age were my friends, but they weren't like Lee Ellen.   They were corncob rough, almost like boys.   Wanda Faye Griggs, whose cornfields we farmed down on the Toccoa River, and Shirley Harper who lived about a half-mile up the Old Epworth Road could both whip me in wrestling, a foot race, or *tag— you're it.*   Wanda Faye chewed tobacco, and once she spit juice in my eye before we fought.

Lee Ellen didn't know it, but I was more than her secret admirer.   She was pretty and smart and most of all, she was friendly to me.   Throughout the eighth grade, I watched her every chance I got.   To me, she was the prettiest girl in the world, but I could never get the courage to talk to her.

Once, I did send her a note and asked her if she liked me.   She returned the note and said she did, but afterwards I lost my nerve, and was too shy to talk with her.   I pondered: *What do you say to a girl after she tells you she likes you?   I mean a real girl like Lee Ellen, not a girl like Wanda Faye or Shirley.   Lee wouldn't want to hear me talk about catching chickens.   And I couldn't tell her those tall tales my chicken catcher buddies told me.   If I did, she'd never like me again.   They were my best buddies, but they cussed like sailors, told crude vulgar jokes, and some of the older ones got drunk when they weren't catching chickens. I was dead sure she wouldn't want to hear about our poker games and the fights some of the gamblers got into, while riding in the back of the old crate to the chicken houses. And, if she knew that some of my chicken catcher buddies had been expelled from school, or sent to reform school and some even were ex- jailbirds, she'd never look my way again.*

I spent the entire eighth grade year in love with her, or so I thought. Infatuated, or maybe it was simply puppy-love. I don't know what it was, but I had it bad. Silently, from a distance I adored everything about her. The mystery of our romance was shared with no one, especially not to her, the perfect girl of my dreams.

After our first year at high school, I wished I had told her how I felt about her. One day I saw her walking down the hall, holding hands with another boy, one much older and bigger than me. That boy had no problem talking to her. Painfully, I watched the girl of my dreams smile at him. Strolling together, they chatted easily. Seeing them so happy together, opened a floodgate of my bad feelings.

What's he doing with my girl? I ranted to myself. Queasiness took hold of my stomach; oddly, at the same time, I felt mad as hell, and I wanted to hit someone, but I didn't. Instead, I turned and gave my locker a furious one-two punch. Now, with sore knuckles, I really felt stupid. Passing students skirted around me, and gawked at me, like I was a mad dog with the mange. My rage stayed and gnawed at me. I felt like a pimple-faced nincompoop, and knew well that in a fight, he'd wipe the floor with me. I wanted to slug the guy whose hand she held. *She's my girl! Don't you know that? Moron!* I wanted to tell him, just before I busted him in the mouth with my sore fist.

My anger moved on and fell next upon my crude chicken catcher buddies. In my fragile state of mind and my twisted thinking, I felt they were to blame for me losing my girl. It was their fault and they would get what was coming to them. I'd get even. Maybe on a cold dark night in a chicken house, I'd throw and crack an egg up against their empty rowdy heads. Or maybe I'd push over and crash a tall stack of chicken coops on them as they walked by. But then I cooled down a bit and realized something. They didn't know anything about my girl. I'd told them nothing about my secret girlfriend.

Finally, and sadly, I accepted the truth. The blame belonged to me. I was a coward for not ever talking to her. I became even more distraught. I wanted to kick myself for having acted like a boy without a tongue. I was deeply in love with her, and *she* had never known it. Now she was some other boy's girl—the lucky guy's name was Tommy Duke. He was now The Duke of Earl and I was nameless.

For weeks I moped around like a sick calf. I'd see them together—*she* and that guy Tommy. But later, I stopped seeing her. She had moved away, I heard, and no one seemed to know where. I would never see her again.

———————

Mom had also moved away that year. She left the farm down on Mill Creek soon after Jerry left home. She went to live with Bill and she worked in the Cagle Poetry Company Hatchery. My step-mom-to-be immediately moved in with us on the farm. She treated me well, but I didn't always get along with her kids. Her son Poncho was younger than I, and was a good kid. We got along well together. He loved living on the farm and never complained about all the work. I taught him how to drive the farm truck. His older sister, Sally, on the other hand, was a pain. No one could get along with her, including her own mom. Eventually she was sent away to live with her older sister in Gastonia, North Carolina.

In the summer of that same year, we had planted and cultivated about thirty acres of corn. It was now time to start gathering the crop, and Poncho and I pulled corn every evening after school until dark. On those few days when it wasn't raining, he and I would get excused from school at mid-day, so we'd have more time to work. Still, the barn wasn't filling up fast enough for Dad, so he told us both to stay out of school the entire next week. I didn't like my dad's demand, but I said nothing. I also read into his demand that he had no plans to allow me to go to school anymore. Not ever again. So, like all my brothers before me, I made plans to leave the farm. I shared those plans with no one.

My sister Peggy had agreed instantly that I could come to live with her and Walter, her husband. No questions asked. I will never forget my escape from the farm. Instead of going to church with the family on Sunday night, I told dad that I needed to do some work in the barn. He agreed. Work trumped everything on the farm, even worship. While everyone went to preaching, I hauled my meager clothes and my other belongings over to Peggy's house using the farm truck. Then I returned the old farm truck, parked it, and I ran away from that dark holler down on Mill Creek. I ran toward a new future.

Forty years later I would learn Lee Ellen Bandy had simultaneously fled her own familiar surroundings. Like me, she had faced a family dilemma. Little did I know back then that our paths would cross once more and that her life would end at the same place where my life had begun—Down on Mill Creek.

———————

Chapter 22 - DAPPLED MORALITY

He was the kind of religious man who made one prefer being around drunks, petty thieves, and trash collectors. Reverend Hoyt Douglas was a dual professional man, both a minister and a high school teacher in Fannin County in the mid 1960s. He thoroughly enjoyed the power and esteem garnered by his cleric collar and that minister sticker on his Volkswagen bug's windshield.

The economy was booming then. Finding qualified personnel to accept low wages to teach high school students was not easy. Fannin County accepted anyone with a college degree. Personality, experience, and people skills were nice but not necessary for a teaching position. Reverend Douglas had none, and they hired him.

In a word, he was arrogant. His educator demeanor and mantra seemed to be, "Teenage students should be seen and never heard." His ministerial demeanor and mantra was, "God's going to get you for that, and I'm going to help him get you."

His professional behavior was contradictory to

his two professions. He had a personal attitude toward life that seemed to be, "Humanity I love. It is students I can't stand." I, Jeff Cagle, a rebellious sophomore with his own problems, was confused by this educator and man of God.

Before meeting Reverend Douglas, I was certain I knew who God was. After enduring his self-righteous presence, I considered maybe I could be wrong and wondered, *Is Reverend Douglas God?* I also questioned God's true nature and how people should treat one another. But, oddly, I sensed something in common with this despicable man: We both were mad as hell about something painful from our past. But unlike me, Reverend Douglas was looking for a dog to kick, something to soothe his sores of the past.

My first encounter with him was during sophomore English. The teacher, Mrs. Ford, like so many teachers back then, was a nervous rookie. She was inexperienced, easily excited by teen group behavior, and far from a profile in courage. She rarely had control of the her class. Often, she was late to class.

In desperation one fall morning, she abandoned her rowdy classroom. We were left unattended, but she assigned a student to make a list of all who talked while she was gone—all classmates easily made the list. She frantically paced to the principal's office seeking help in restoring order to her classroom.

During her absence, Reverend Douglas entered our room of rowdiness. With a voice sounding like nails being dragged down a chalkboard, he demanded, "SILENCE!"

All students quickly complied, but the Reverend wanted more than silence. He took it upon himself to find one student to pay penance. An example would be made of the student. For the sacrificial goat, he chose the most shy, least talkative boy in the class, Marc "Smiley" Campbell.

Now Marc said little for a good reason. This boy stuttered and his face was slightly distorted. At the right end, where his tight lips met and merged, his lips hooked upward. It gave him an apparent constant slight smile or a smirk, depending on your point of view. The Reverend did not like the smiling student. Unaware of Marc's facial deformity, he began his tirade:

"Oh, you think this ruckus is funny, do you?"

Befuddled, Marc shrugged his shoulders, but gave no response.

"Get that stupid smirk off your face, pretty boy. Right now!"

Marc's eyes widened as he sheepishly looked up at the Reverend, permanent smile unchanged, he faintly stuttered his serious words, "ma...ma...ma... me?" Some guys in our class broke out in laughter. Most all the girls sensed the misunderstanding, but Reverend Douglas did not. One girl near Marc tried to explain the situation to him, but he turned toward her, pointed his finger at her, and said, "If I want anything out of you, I'll tell you. For now, keep your mouth shut, and work on your assignment."

He then walked to Marc, reached and grabbed his upper arm and lifted him from his chair. He told him, "You come with me, young man."

Seeing the Reverend's error I felt I couldn't take any more. I rose from my desk and muttered, "You got it wrong, man. Lay off Smiley." John Doperalski, a brute of a youngster and our football team's largest player even as a sophomore, shoved me back in my seat. "Sit down. He'll get you kicked off the team if you try stopping him." The Reverend cut his scornful eyes at me, but said nothing and continued toward the door with Marc.

Mrs. Ford re-entered the class, but with no principal in tow. Seeing Marc being escorted by the Reverend, she asked, "Where are you taking him?"

"I'll tell you later. This student is acting disrespectful."

In the hallway, a sermon was preached to Marc regarding respect. We heard the demeaning message our classmate endured. We all shamefully cringed when three licks of the "Board of Education" were administered by the Reverend.

Apple-faced and head bowed, Smiley re-entered the classroom. The entire class felt humiliated and powerless. When Mrs. Ford began to teach, we heard little. Frustrated and angry, I couldn't decide who I was most disgusted with, myself or the Reverend. I sat and attacked myself: *Why didn't you do something? You're a big bad football player, but you didn't stop him. You did nothing to prevent that bully from badgering an innocent classmate! Who are you, really, Jeff Cagle? Are you a boy of a man? You are a coward!*

My guilt lingered, and it was a long time before I could look my classmates in the eyes again. Mrs. Ford read my passive behavior as studiousness, but my grades in her English class proved otherwise. Like

Reverend Douglass' misjudgment of Smiley Campbell, her assessment, too, had been flawed. I responded to both errors with malicious acts.

———

In high school I liked things that went *BANG!* Loud noise was a rebellious teen's cure for small town boredom and the injustice of the lords of discipline— imperfect teachers. In that regard, I was no different from many of my peers. Some students took action. We devised our own ways for chasing away rural life's malaise and settling the score. These actions sometimes ran afoul of the law.

The tag on his gray uniform shirt read Trooper Darby. He was the trooper whose cruiser I had thrown a Cherry Bomb firecracker under on one Saturday night. Just for fun, a few football teammates and I were drinking beer and driving around. We were neither stupid nor irresponsible. We had rules. The driver could not drink.

I had a sack full of Cherry Bomb firecrackers. With them, we tested the withstand capability of the Atlanta Constitution Newspaper Tubes at select teachers' residences. *What a clever thing to do,* I recall thinking then.

Trooper Darby did not think the same. He stopped our fun. Not knowing it was a "Fuzz-mobile" that had pulled over our driver, I lit and threw the Cherry Bomb under it. After the smoke cleared, with gun in hand, the trooper slowly and cautiously got out of the cruiser. He demanded that each of us exit the vehicle and place our hands in the air. He took possession of my sack of fire crackers, but didn't arrest anyone. Trooper Darby was firm, but understanding. He told us, "Go home! If any one of you renegades crosses my path again, I'll throw you under the jail." We did as he told us.

————————

The Reverend Douglas flexed his authoritative muscles again in Mrs. Ford's classroom. It was about two weeks after the embarrassing incident with Marc. She was again late getting to class. It had almost become her modus operandi. My football teammates devised a plan. We felt some glory and fanfare was appropriate to announce her late arrival on this particular day. It would be a day neither she nor her entire class would ever forget.

John Doperalksi was the sergeant at arms for the classroom during the execution of the plan. He took his position in the class doorway, and in a booming voice shouted, "Listen up morons. Shut your mouths.

We're going to play a little trick on Mrs. Ford. Keep your mouths shut until she gets to class. Not a word, hear me? Study! And after it's over, not a word to anyone about what you saw happen. I mean no one! Not a word." He then began slamming his gigantic fist into his other gigantic palm, suggesting the consequences.

While 'Doper' kept watch, cat-quick I lay on the floor and constructed an "arrival fanfare" bomb. First, Mrs. Ford's chair was carefully slid under her desk, so she would have to tug it out when she came to class. Second, between the chair's and desk's legs I neatly inserted and tied ten party poppers. When she moved the chair, the BANG would be triggered.

With job completed, I up-righted myself and took my seat. The entire classroom remained quiet as a morgue. We waited for Mrs. Ford's traditional late arrival.

When she entered the classroom, a suspicious look flashed across her face. The class's unusual somberness had made her perplexed. She stopped, scanned the room of studious classmates, but then toggled her head and marched over to her desk. The chair was tugged.

In the dead silence, the ten party poppers

sounded like three sticks of dynamite going off.   The sound resonated up the hallway.   Mrs. Ford's face turned waxy gray and she stumbled backwards, holding a hand over her heart. Some classmates yelled, "SURPRISE!"

Out of nowhere, Reverend Douglas appeared in our classroom. He stood in the doorway and emphatically screeched, "Who set off those firecrackers?"   He did not acknowledge Mrs. Ford, who trembled and leaned weak-kneed against the block wall under a small American flag. She stared at the floor, trying to regain her composure and to restore her breathing pattern. Soon she looked up and assured Reverend Douglas, "I'm okay. I can handle this. You can go." But, he parked his boney body in the doorway and stayed.

With color restored to her face, Mrs. Ford stepped forward, tilted her head down then up, and told us, "Don't anyone move from your seat."   She assertively approached the intercom speaker, blinked her eyes continuously, and issued a feeble plea for the principal to come to her classroom.   She then moved back and stood under the small American flag with her arms crossed. She went nowhere near her desk and chair.

The principal told the class that no one could enter or leave the room until someone confessed to setting off the firecrackers. We spent the entire day inside the same class, with only individual escorted bathroom breaks. No one confessed. At the end of the day, the principal told the class we were to return to the same classroom tomorrow, for a repeat of the day. We would remain there until someone came forward and confessed.

The next day, classroom changes returned to normal. Students transitioned and attended all their usual classes. Someone had given me up with a phone call to the principal. Another had corroborated the story. I received ten "Board of Education" licks and was suspended from school for three days. Reverend Douglas delighted in witnessing all ten licks.

The last time I saw Reverend Douglas alive was in late winter of my sophomore year. A light coat of snow blanketed him. Blowing sleet pinged his vehicle and pelted his still body as it blew through the busted out windshield of his wrecked Volkswagen bug. He lay semiconscious, dying. His head and face were streaked with blood, his right forearm was splintered, and the bone stuck out through his skin and shirt. He sporadically jerked and uttered a groan. In the passenger side floorboard, a half-empty Southern Comfort bottle.

An early morning storm had hit. School in Fannin County had been called off, but the announcement had been slow in getting to the radio station for broadcasting. The accident happened on Highway 5, just about one hundred yards short of the high school's entrance. His speeding VW bug had struck the rear of a snow plow truck. No one else was injured.

Three football teammates and I stood and watched him die. Frozen rain and sleet struck us as a siren from a State Trooper's cruiser pierced the quiet, frigid, air. Later we heard a different siren, an approaching ambulance.

We left the scene seconds prior to the State Trooper's arrival. I'd broken no law, but since the firecracker incident, keeping my distance from all law enforcement seemed wise. I pulled my old fifty-four Ford into the high school entrance drive, turned around, and headed back toward McCaysville. My teammates were wordless. Inside my car, it was as somber as a freshly dug grave.

Homeward bound, out the window we all stole another glance at the accident scene. Passing by quickly, we noted that the trooper looked familiar. He was the same trooper whose cruiser I had thrown a Cherry Bomb under on that fall Saturday night,

Trooper Darby.

Seeing a man die changed me. I did not like Reverend Douglas. There was little to like. But I didn't want to see him dead. I actually knew nothing about him, the cause for his darkness of heart, his yesterdays' storms. I felt he meant well, but had allowed his bitter past to swallow up all his compassion.

Seeing ice swarm and assault his struggling body made me aware of how fragile my own life was. It made me reflect more on the world around me. I thought about life's unfairness, its cruelty, and its lack of meaning. *Why had God allowed a minister to die, but let me continue to live?* I pondered.

Also, I wondered about the trooper whose responsibility it was to handle the cleanup and bring order to the Reverend's ironic death. *How do you reconcile others' contradictory behavior and brazen contempt?* The question lingered in my mind.

In my eyes, Trooper Darby became a tall man that night he gave me a pass and didn't throw me in jail for the firecracker incident. He grew even taller that morning I saw him protect and serve in the freezing rain at the wreck site of a dead minister.

I, too, grew from what I witnessed my sophomore year in Fannin County. Some English was learned from Mrs. Ford. She taught me grammar, sentence structure, and the importance of using correct language. But, life lessons more important were learned in her class. She taught that doing the right thing is never easy, failures are frequent, and doing what's right is often poorly rewarded. Before the year was over, I learned from her that love's labor is never lost.

My James Dean rebel persona passed away. Forgive and forget became my new mantra. New ways to deal with boredom were discovered—academics and work. I matured and became a more responsible young man.

————————

THE
GOLDEN
YEARS

PART III

2006- Late Spring

"When I was fourteen I was falling fast
For a blue eyed girl in my Homeroom class
Tryin' to find the courage to ask her out
Was like tryin' to get oil from a water spout

And what she would've said I can't say
I never did ask and she moved away
But I learned something from my blue eyed girl
Sink or swim you've got to give it a whirl

Life's a dance you learn as you go
Sometimes you lead, sometimes you follow
Don't worry 'bout what you don't know
Life's a dance you learn as you go."

From "Life's A Dance" by John Michael Montgomery

"I need me a mountain to rest my eyes against."

By Earnest Smith, father of author *Lee Smith*

Chapter 23 - A FRESH RAIN

Straight-faced, Lee sat in the dusky room sipping bitter drive-thru coffee. Scurrying about in the backrooms, and yelling back and forth to each other in boisterous and almost accusatory tones, the realty agents hadn't heard her slip in the front door and take a seat. From an old rocker beside the fire hearth she half-listened and then half-smiled. The ruckus encouraged her, brought hope, and oddly gave her solace—problems were being resolved; things made clear; something she'd be doing soon with her new life.

Looking up at the waiting room's high ceiling made her feel free. Threatened a bit, but free. Free for what? Her forced early retirement came with no to-do list and its basis was bogus. PTSD was something those other bleeding heart law enforcement officers had, the ones who whined about their poor childhood. "Not my circus. Not my monkey," she had told herself.

The fireplace's chimney, a randomly piled-to-the-ceiling wall of fieldstones, was safe, secure, and permanent. The room's smell—that of aged wood smoke and baked dirt—returned Lee to her youth. All was so natural then—musty, earthy, even dank, but lasting and as real as God himself. Columns of wood ash dust channeled at an angle from the fireplace. Lee logged the familiar bygone environment as a miracle cure for all that ailed her, but today's technology driven, ecology friendly people would label her belief as rabbit's-foot faith.

Even though rain had fallen all night, dust drifted in columns. She noticed the orderly pattern. Ensuring *order* had been her life's sole purpose. Silently in her murky mind she enunciated the word: *Orrrrrr derrrrrr. Order is a good thing*, she told herself? *Law is order, and good law is good order,* she clearly recalled once hearing a judge charge the jury.

Slanted sunrays filtered through the screen door's grid and were the true cause of the seeming order. Still, the room was murky, and the light beams converged to form dappled images on the wall. These images were evanescent. Orderly they faded and drifted away. Like raccoon eyes, the pitch-black knots on the pine paneling stole peeks at the feather colored boarded floor.

Candles on either end of the rough-hewn mantle were starved for air. Fluttering and struggling to stay lit, they too cast moving objects, but only on the ceiling. As though a man's hands shaped and guided them, the silhouettes migrated aimlessly, but converged and vanished at the ceiling's peak.

Outside, slow, time-spaced rainwater dripped from the porch eaves. Sporadically, drops fell in puddles below, splashing and rippling. A heavy fog lifted from behind and floated over the blue mountain range. Closer by, a young crow faintly cawed and a mockingbird coincidentally mimicked three other birds. Both flapped away when two pups trotted across the parking lot's coarse rain-rinsed gravel. They nipped and bit at each other, not watching nor caring where they were going, but seemingly in a hurry to get there. One yelped, lost his footing, and tumbled nose first into the gravel. Then another yelp—sharp and more ear piercing than the first. Like the crack of gunfire, it snipped and zipped through the fresh morning air.

Balancing her coffee in hand, Lee rose from the rocker, and walked to the entrance to check out the curious racket. Gently she swung open the screen door, but didn't look at the brawling blue-ticks. A beautiful rainbow arcing from behind the now sun-lit mountain range demanded her attention. Frozen in time she stood mesmerized and remembered promises. First, God's to humanity concerning life, death, floods, and destruction. Then the one she had made to herself, to return to her mountains.

"Yes, can I help you," asked a thin fox-faced man with a beaked nose and receding hairline. A thirtyish full-figured woman wearing plum colored lipstick stood behind him with her hands on her hips. She smiled like a sunflower, making her presence and her pearly teeth known.

"Oh, yes. Yes, I hope you can. My name is Lee Ellen Cornwell. I called yesterday about the cabin property."

"Sure. Sure. Sure. Miz Cornwell." Holding out a dead-fish limp hand he said, "I'm Bruce Foster. Won't you please come inside?" Lee did not shake his hand, and he didn't realize she had already waited inside the dimly lit waiting room for over five minutes.

He continued, "I apologize for our dark office this morning. On second thought maybe we ought to just step out on the porch until the electrician gets here to get our power back on. There'll be light out there. You see, lightning apparently knocked off our power, our computers, and everything else in our offices during that terrible electrical storm we had early this morning."

The three moved out onto the front porch that fully spanned the cabin's front. Hearing them, the two pups immediately ran toward the cabin. Seeing them approach, Mr. Foster's assistant jutted backwards and returned to the office. They leaped up the porch steps in two bounds. Excited and rambunctious, their nails scratched the wooden porch floor. One stood on its hind-legs and placed its paws on Lee's stomach. Smelling and licking her hands, it then went back to all fours. Mr. Foster was loved on next. With twitching shoulders and pursed lips nearly touching the screen door, his assistant's wide open eyes kept tabs on the playful dogs.

Lee didn't flinch. She was still awe-struck and lost in the beauty. Again she gazed at the rising fog, the rainbow, and the mountains in the background. Dog paws, even clingy claws, and wet licks to her hands didn't affect her. During her almost thirty years in law enforcement, she had once been assigned to the K-9 investigative division. There she learned these assumed to be crude actions were merely a dog's data gathering technique. She understood dogs and knew they always had your back. In a pinch, they could be more trusted than some of her fellow law enforcement friends.

Mr. Foster first cajoled and, waving his pale lanky arms, tried shooing the pups away. To Lee's dislike, he then kicked them. He yelled at them, "Get out of here, you mangy mutts. Don't you come back neither."

They howled, stuck their tails between their legs, and slinked away. Through the gravel they first trotted, then galloped, and went back to nipping at each other. Like nothing had happened, they sped away as though late for an important meeting up the road.

"Now, Miz Cornwell, if I remember correctly, you were looking for some property you could build a cabin on, and you are moving here from the Atlanta area. Is that correct?"

"Yes, that's right. What I'm interested in is just a few acres of land with a nice view of the mountains. On water is nice, but not necessary. I want a place where I can rest my eyes on the mountains."

"I see. Well, I think we have exactly what you are looking for. We have some land that has not been developed yet. Years ago the property was a dairy farm and later it was just a farm. A creek runs through it. And, it does have a nice view of mountains on both sides of a long meadow. But now I must tell you in advance that this property doesn't have much in the way of utilities. No treated water, no city sewer, no garbage pickup, or paved roads." He quickly added, "That will keep your taxes low. But, it's not like anything in Atlanta. If you want those things, you'll have to get them for yourself."

"That won't be a problem. You see, I once lived here in Fannin County. It was way out in the sticks and a long time ago, but I remember what it's like. I'll re-adjust to mountain life."

"Okay. I just wanted you to know upfront, because you see, the property I have in mind for you hasn't had anyone living on it in over twenty years. We at Foster Realty were fortunate. We bought the farm a few years back when the developer's loan fell through. He had big plans for that property. He was going to turn the farm property into a resort with a lake, a golf course, and a gated community with a few high dollar houses. We've been holding on to it, waiting for the economy to turn around."

He then shaded his eyes with one hand held to his creased forehead. He looked directly at a mud-colored jeep in the parking lot and said, "I tell you what. Rather than me trying to tell you about it, I think it would be best if I just drove you up there to the old farm in my jeep and let you look at it for yourself. How's that sound?"

"Sounds good to me. I'm ready when you are."

"Let me leave some instructions for that electrician who's coming to get the power back on."

Pointing out into the parking lot, he told Lee, "We'll go there in my old jeep. Roads there may be washed out a little after all that hard rain we had. Go ahead and get in. I'll be right back and we'll go down to Mill Creek."

———————

The old Kaiser jeep was not like what she expected. It was surprisingly clean. Inside and out, this vintage Willeys Woody had been restored to its original newness. The scent of leather seats spilled out, wafted about, stirring Lee's memory when she opened its door.

His name was ...? Oh, yeah, it belonged to that jerk, Jim—Mr. Football jock, the one who drowned himself in English Leather cologne; the one who dumped me like I was a bad habit my junior year at Sibley High. She stalled a second reflecting before climbing inside the jeep. Stepping up and scooting across the seat she consoled herself: *Oh well, that was yesterday and yesterday's gone. Live and learn. Die and forget it all.*

It was spotless—no dust, mud, or spilled coffee in sight anywhere, not even a gum wrapper on the midnight black floor-mats. On the dashboard, Lee saw an old companion—a CB radio. More memories rolled in. This time they were from her early years in law enforcement, the days before smart phones and the even smarter tech savvy drug dealers. Back then, she'd monitor emergencies to stay ahead of what was coming up, enabling a quick response to her sworn duty to protect and serve. She wanted to power it up and listen in, but didn't. Instead she stared at it and reminisced about those days and also about Fannin County, the place of her youth that she hardly recognized today.

Lee heard feet crunching gravel and looked up to see Mr. Foster nearing her. Noting her eyes fixed on the CB, he said, "Oh, I see you like my antique communications system." He then slammed the door and glanced in the jeep's rear view mirror. "Well, I'll tell you something Miz Cornwell about these mountains before you move here." Holding up his iPhone and making a twisting motion with it he continued "These things aren't near as smart up here in the mountains as they are down around Atlanta. You can't always get a signal in these hills and hollers. That's why I hung on to my CB. Got me a scanner in the office, too."

"Oh, I see." She didn't bother to tell him that a CB radio also didn't always work well when used in the canyons of tall buildings in downtown Atlanta.

He cranked the jeep, backed up, and eased out to the road's edge. Pulling onto Highway 5 and looking in his rear view mirror again, he asked, "Miz Cornwell, you mentioned that you had lived here as a child. Who did you tell me your folks were here in Fannin?"

"I did not say." He tilted his head, now listening intently. All he heard was the jeep's transmission grinding and its knobby tires rolling toward the Tennessee line. Nervously, he pulled at his beaklike nose and announced "Now where this land is located is in the northern part of the county. It's up near McCaysville. That's still in the mountains, but not so many people live up there anymore. Do you remember McCaysville?"

"Oh sure, I remember it. It's near Copperhill, Tennessee, where the mines are."

"Well, not anymore. The copper played out and they don't mine there now. When I moved here about twenty-five years ago, they shut down those mines. Said it cost too much to get the ore out of the ground. Most all the people that lived and worked there moved away. Not much left today, just rusty shells of chemical plants, pine trees, and kudzu. That stuff now covers up all those once barren red hills. The property I'm going to show you is miles from there. It's out in the country."

"Oh, I see." Lee knew more about the area

than she'd led Mr. Foster to think. As a former law enforcement officer she learned early on to volunteer no information to strangers. So far, Mr. Foster was a stranger.

Her law enforcement experience had also taught her that unless on duty, never let others know that you work in law enforcement. To do so can set one up for threats and unwanted special favor requests. Favors like, "Officer Cornwell, can you make this speeding ticket go away? Twenty dollars might come your way." Also, there were those annoying requests from people who mistook law enforcement personnel for attorneys— always asking questions about the interpretation of the law. Those requests usually centered around one question: "How can I skirt a law that somehow has inconvenienced me?" To them, their friend in law enforcement was just a free get out of jail pass. Lastly, there were those so called friends who bragged about having you as a friend in law enforcement. They were nothing more than ego addicts. They saw a law enforcement friend as a cheap and easy ego hit when they introduced you to their friends.

Whatever their angle, Lee saw no upside to friendships with non-law-enforcement people. It was a one-way street. They always wanted something. They made her feel she was a pawn on *their* chessboard.

Consequently, she limited her friendships to only people with whom she shared things in common. That meant members of the fraternity of law enforcement. They were her real friends. They understood.

"Do you recognize this place here?" he asked as they drove past Mercier's Apple Orchard. "Did you know that next to Stone Mountain Georgia, Mercier's has the most visitors of any place in Georgia?"

"Well, no... and no. I mean, I do remember an apple orchard, but it looked nothing like this when I lived here as a kid." A confused looked crossed her face and she said, "Where are all these buses and cars going?"

"Oh they're going to Mercier's Apple Shed or to ride through the orchard in an apple wagon. People travel here from everywhere just to shop at Mercier's."

"Hmm?" Then with a bit of ire tingeing her voice she informed Mr. Foster, "Well, this is exactly what I'm trying to get away from—traffic and shoppers and wall-to-wall people!"

"Well, this property I'll show you today is nothing like this. It's quiet as a graveyard down there on that old farm. In fact, there is only one other person who now lives there. Oh, that reminds me. I need to make a call."

Holding the iPhone in one hand he looked down and attempted to thumb-key in the numbers. Suddenly he looked up and slammed on the brakes. "Holy shit!" he shrieked while pounding his hand on the jeep's horn button. "Meep-Meep...Meep-Meep" recurred the strange, but familiar horn sound as smoke boiled up from the jeep's skidding tires. They were within inches from the tail end of a chartered bus with a Florida tag.

Lee urgently offered, "Let me make your call for you Mr. Foster. You drive. I'll key the numbers. Just call them out to me. It might save you a 1050 and a jump in your insurance cost."

Slightly put off by the suggestion, he shrugged his shoulders and grudgingly handed his smart phone to Lee.   Faster than an auctioneer he fired off the number, "706-555-6322. Let me have it when you're done."

Taking the cell phone from Lee's hands he snarled and said, "Hello! Is this Jeff? Are you to my office yet? Well, I see. Now there's one other thing I need for you to fix after you get the power back on. It's that dang security system. It keeps going off at all hours of the day and night. The sheriff's guys come out when it goes off and I get charged a fee. Can you look at it and see why it's not working right? If you don't see anything that's causing the problem, then just turn it off. It's more trouble than it's worth. No one in Fannin County is going to break into my little office, for Pete's sake."

Mr. Foster, calmer now, stopped talking, listened briefly and then said, "Okay. I'll see you back at my office a little after noon. Bye."

"That's the electrician who's coming to get my power back on at my office. He's like you. He once lived here in Fannin County. He moved back here a while back and he does electrical work now. He's a pretty good egg. Oh, by the way. He lives down here where we're going. He has a little cabin down on Mill Creek. Y'all might be neighbors some day if you decide you like this property I'm going to show you." He turned his head toward Lee and winked.

"Okay?" Lee gave a straight-faced smile, crinkled her brow, wondering why Mr. Foster had shared all the superfluous information.

Traveling on toward McCaysville, Lee saw many places that looked vaguely familiar. The road that turned off to Granny's old house, she recognized well. She'd lived there with Granny as a kid and would never forget her. A sick feeling burned in the pit of her stomach as unsettling memories swamped her mind. She didn't want to think about them. She shook her head vigorously from side to side. Then attempting to rid the unpleasant memories from her mind, she uncharacteristically blurted out: "Mr. Foster, where did you move from, to Fannin County?"

"Oh, I'm like about half the people who live in Fannin County today. I'm from the north, Lexington, Kentucky by way of Port Charlotte, Florida. The locals call us Half-Backs. We're from the north, but we moved to Florida to escape the snow and the cold. Then we decided we didn't like the heat either, so we compromised and moved halfway back home—to north Georgia where we have four seasons. I love it here." He then pulled at his thin nose again. For a second she studied the expression on his face. It didn't match the tone of his words or his body language.

"Oh ... I see."

Pointing up the highway with his right index finger he then said, "Okay Miz Cornwell. We're turning left at that restaurant you see ahead. Soon we'll be on a gravel road. You see on your right up there where those condos are? Well, the older local folks here tell me there was once a drive-in theater there. Now that's something you don't see every day, do you? Drive your car in, park it and sit in your car watching a movie on a giant white outside screen."

"Uh huh," Lee muttered and glanced out the window as they drove by. "How far is it from here to where we are turning off?"

"Not far. We're turning here." Gearing down the jeep, he gave no turn signal, but made a quick left-hand turn.

"It's only about two more miles on down to the old farm. We'll be crossing a creek in a few minutes, but you won't get wet." He grinned as the old Woody descended the gravel road.

Gearing down and slowing to a crawl, they splashed across a small spring branch. Then they motored down a muddy road for about a half-mile. Mill Creek came into sight. It flowed through a meadow, just as he had said, but today it wasn't peaceful. Its curious troubled waters captured Lee's ears. The old Woody stopped. Mr. Foster parked between two tall pines.

"This is it. Get out and we'll walk a short distance to where the lot is. I think you'll like it. What do you think about the mountains surrounding this place?"

"Yes. I think this might work." Looking from side to side, she then said, "It's a little more grown up and in the rough than I had imagined, but with some clearing off, my cabin may fit in here nicely."

Briars grabbed at their legs as they walked toward the lot. Breathing misty morning air, she scanned the mountains, the soaked green fields, and the giant oaks, bark blackened by rain.

Turning and churning, Mill Creek's rain-swollen and muddied waters cried out questions to Lee, *Who are you and why are you here?*

She pondered, *Am I home? Is this where I belong?* Her refuge-seeking mind scrambled for answers.

Chapter 24 - YOU CAN'T GO HOME AGAIN

"Is it not strange when one is a kid in
a little town, all that you think and dream
about is somehow getting to the great city.
And when one reaches my present doddering
age, he begins to dream fondly of the green
pastures again—of finding a nice cool spot on
top of some fairly convenient mountain...... .
. All that I want is a comfortable cabin with a
front porch—and lots of shade."

Thomas Wolfe, Author

Outside a sleazy café, kamikaze-like bugs wheeled, bombed, and hissed about a buzzing streetlight. Above this dive's front window flickered a red neon *OPEN* sign. A bell tinkled and a rancid scent escaped each time its warped glass door swiveled and squeaked. Cops, pavement princesses, and just-off-the-greyhound folks retreated here.

It was a sultry Monday night. Fighting fatigue, near the back at a booth taking a coffee break, sat Lee with Jim Moore, a fellow Atlanta policeman. The lighting was poor inside, but behind a long counter a squatty, toothless, wrinkled-faced waitress worked frantically. She balanced and buttered toast on her nub of an arm.

"Jim, I'm tired ... You got a Tums on you?" Four shaky fingers went across her mouth, muffling a belch. "Maybe I'm too tired to make a decision this big." He tapped a silver foiled roll and stood it upright on the table. Lee removed the foil and placed the hard tablet on her tongue. She crunched it. Fumbling with the roll she said, "Everybody's talking ... talking loud and saying nothing." Her sleepless eyes then froze on Jim's shield. She muttered, "I'm numb, Jim—just mentally and emotionally spent."

Slow, like Indian winter crawling toward fall, her eyes moved. At the entrance she noted a few bugs migrating from the streetlight to the picture window. She heisted her chipped cup, and it hovered over the sticky table top. Her gaze fixed on the window-bashing bugs. Two bar-seated customers rose, looked over their shoulders, and cast furtive glances at Lee as they walked. The door bell tinkled—two street girls going to sell tail.

Jim yawned into his fist. Lee received his convict-in-the-yard stare— empty eyes wide open, but not curious. Her shoulders were stiff as their starched blues.

Her trusted friend had heard it all before.   A thirty-two year veteran, hell, he'd probably said the same words at least once himself.   Both he and Lee had lifeguarded society's cesspool for maybe too long. Lee's words were said by all cops if they stayed.   Many didn't.   The average swim time in the cesspool was about seven years.   After that, they transferred to a desk job, worked for security companies, or left.   A few who overstayed ate their gun.

The chipped cup came closer to her faded face. She pondered: *Why don't they get it?   They refuse to understand or care what law enforcement life is like. Maybe like cocaine—that CSI bullshit Hollywood doses out slow-rots their brain.   I wish John Q would accept the truth.   I got to rabbit out of here and find me another hole to jump in.   I gotta.*

The culprit and pathology didn't change—a gradual contempt for the human condition.   Every cop eventually grew into it.   Familiarity bred contempt, and cops got to know their clientele better than they ever wanted to.

In the concrete arena, the "usual suspects" were under-educated, and under everything.   When they opened their mouths, they lied.   They stole, they raped, and they killed.   Every day exposure to the perps made most cops reject altruistic philosophies. Daily they saw man's inhumanity to man. The daily dose paralyzed feelings. But Lee hadn't met with her friend Jim to cry in coffee and discuss Nihilistic philosophy. She opened up and ranted:

"Jim, I'm serious. No secret, I'm burnt out. How do *you* do it? I mean how do you *not* get tired of nothing ever making sense? The politics— the Blue Code cover ups—brass hiding other brass's screw ups?"

"I didn't tell you the real reason I'm thinking about it ..., taking early retirement. I owe it to you. You've been there for me, listening. Always there."

"Yeah, that's about all I'm good for nowadays— listening. Too old to chase even a busting slack druggie. Can't getter done no more, Lee." He mockingly rubbed back his receding steely-gray hair. "Yeah, I could grow me a ponytail. Do some social work, maybe. Think I could be one of those collared confessional priests?" He forced a chuckle meant to gauge Lee's mood, her level of blue-suit-blues. Lee stared. His laugh trailed away. The space between them got quieter than an empty jail cell. Jim's radio blared a code 21. His big knuckled hand reached for the knob and squelched the volume.

A waitress cut a dash up to them. Her brown

bony hand held forward a coffee pot. She brushed back her hair, put a curt smile on her mule face, and asked, "Warm you up, officers? Hey! Today's y'all's lucky day. She pointed to the sign on the glass window. In sun-faded ink, now robin's egg blue, it read 'National Doughnut Day.' "Cops get 'em free. What say I bring y'all a couple hot glazed ones to share?"

Thumbing his stomach with a faint fixed smile, Jim responded, "Thank you, but no. I'm watching my figure. I'll take some coffee though."

Lee dismissed her with a hand wave. Topping off Jim's cup, the server turned, tilted back her head, and popped her gum. Coffee pot out front, she appeared to be pulled and led by it as she glided away muttering, "Cops—full of themselves. Always full of themselves!"

Lee's head sagged. Close to tears, she jammed her knuckles against her mouth. Then her head popped up. She urged her eyes to make contact with Jim's and said, "I want to tell you something. I've told no one, and I know you'll keep this to yourself. It's Captain Davis. He's why I want out early. His office politics and cover-ups." Lee's trembling fingertips caressed the widow's peak of her frayed graying hair. She paused and then said, "I can't take it anymore. And if I stay on, he as same as told me I'll have to testify against that piece of crap, Sergeant Welch."

"Sorry, timeout. What's Welch got to do with you retiring? Heck, Welch got knocked back to desk work years ago, back when he was suspended for roughing up that rock dealing kid over on MLK."

"Right, but Davis is really trying to stick it to Welch this time. He wants to limit his retirement package. If I testify against Welch, Davis thinks Welch will be busted back again, lower his pay grade and retirement. Could leave him less than half his full retirement. That's if he's not acquitted."

"Acquitted? Acquitted for what? What's Davis' got on Welch?"

"Well, a female officer says he sexually assaulted her. That's why Davis wants *me* to testify. You see, twelve years ago I was..." Lee looked away, but continued, "I ... I was assaulted by Welch. I reported it. Oh, I reported it. And later, three other ladies in blue reported the creep was doing the same to them. I filed a report and asked Davis to do an investigation. He wore out three pairs of shoes dragging his feet on my complaint. He simply refused to do anything about it."

Jim sat up straight and shoved back his glasses.

"So, what was Welch's bargaining chip? What favors did Davis owe him?" His eyes grew more intense. He quickly quizzed, "And why did Davis stonewall your request?"

"He had no chips, but he had something Davis wanted more—recognition. Davis wanted to go down as the Lone Ranger, the guy in charge of single-handedly cleaning up the drug problem over on MLK and Sweet Auburn. Welch is a pervert and a jerk, but he did have a solid plan. See what I'm saying?"

Jim pushed back his glasses again. The door tinkled. Another working girl entered and took a bar stool.

"Well, not yet, but go on."

"Davis didn't want Welch's plan to be forfeited even if it meant ignoring the complaints of me and three other ladies. You see? Welch had the goods on how to shut down that drug traffic over there. Davis knew he would get a step up in rank if shackled perps from Sweet Auburn made the evening news. All that was needed was for John Q to see those rock mules and the heavyweights all taking a walk. And they did, if you remember. Problem for Welch was, the news camera caught Welch beating up on one. The news amped up the story and spun it into a race issue. News was slow that week and the beating stayed on TV several days. Davis suspended Welch and told the media that *he* had been the master mind behind that drug bust over in the hood."

Jim flicked his chin whiskers with his fingernails.

"Yeah ... sounds about right, but still—where is the motive for stiffing Welch now that he's near retirement? That's all ancient history. Is there money involved?"

"Bingo. You got it, Jim. There is a large chunk of change riding on the outcome of the countersuit Welch now has against the station. The key person called out in the countersuit's bill of particulars is Davis. Their lawyers have tried to settle out of court, but Welch refuses to take a fifty thousand dollar going away settlement. Welch wants the full retirement package he would have received had Davis not knocked him out of the picture during that drug bust. It's going to court and now Davis wants me to come and testify as a character witness against Welch. Hard to tell which one of these two 'heroes' is the tallest pygmy." Lee smirked, twisted her face, and continued, "But, I'm not hanging around to see the winner pinned with a medal. That S.O.B. Davis wouldn't cover our backs when we were being treated like street whores by Welch. And now!" Lee's face reddened and neck splotches popped up as she continued. "Now he has the nerve to ask me to come and testify against Welch to save the city a few dollars. Both of them can go straight to Hell!"

Near tears, Lee bowed her head and lamented, "Jim, I'm just tired—tired of being screwed by people who are supposed to have my back. Anymore, I can't tell the good guys from the bad guys. I'm just tired Jim. So, I'm getting out. I've looked at a place. It's so far back in the mountains that Juan Valdez and his coffee mule couldn't find it."

Smiling through her fought back tears, she continued, "No law enforcement person will ever find me there. If they can't find me, they can't subpoena me to appear at a ridiculous court hearing between Davis and Welch."

She paused, regained her composure, and peered into Jim's now fully attentive eyes. She meekly asked, "What do you think about this, Jim?"

Jim was not a man known to shoot from the hip. He didn't answer at first, but instead held up and directed his coffee cup toward the waitress two tables over. She quickly responded, filled his cup, and asked again, "Are you two sure you wouldn't care for doughnuts? They're free!"

She slinked away, following the coffee pot's lead as the door tinkled again.

Clinking his spoon against the cup as he stirred his coffee, Jim mulled over Lee's comments. His loss of a son in Desert Storm had made him more sensitive, more human. Lee reflected, *He's like Granny. Always thinking, thinking, thinking, and then taking the right action.* This time Jim didn't ponder long.

"Lee, let me ask you a couple of things. Where is your son now? Is he out of Iraq yet?"

"No. He's still there. Won't be out for another six months. Told me he may be a career man. He likes the army life."

"Well, what about your ex-husband? Is he out of the pen yet? Do you ever see him?"

"Don't know. Hope I never see the S.O.B.! He was doing a dime when I had him sent away, but they linked him to some other drug related stuff and tacked on another nickel to his time."

"You see where I'm going don't you? Lee, I know

you love those mountains, but do you really want to live up there alone?"

"Oh, I feel safe there. Jim, I was raised in those mountain woods. Safer there than out on these streets of Atlanta." She tilted her head and nodded toward the café's entrance.

With certitude and sounding serious as a heart attack, he said, "I see you've given this some thought. You've got an action plan. Go for it Officer Cornwell."

———————

Chapter 25 - OLD GOLD

The signed document lay on his desk. Mr. Foster clicked his pen then stood up and proudly said, "Good as gold! This will work just fine and save you some lawyer expense." Atop a file cabinet behind him a digital clock flashed 12:00 continuously. Nodding his hair-challenged bullet head at the agreement, he handed the pen to Lee and said, "Just need your signature, Miz Cornwell.

She scanned the contract, took the pen and signed it. Lee had purchased three acres of land on Mill Creek. Curbing a smile, she nimbly reached in her bag, retrieved an already written check, and slid the earnest money across the desk to Mr. Foster. He scooped it up and said, "Thank you, Miz Cornwell. It's a pleasure doing business with you."

All that was needed now was a title search, something she could do herself at the Blue Ridge courthouse, but felt better having an attorney do it. Mr. Foster had emphatically assured her the plot was unencumbered. "No lien's ever been placed on the property. Foster Realty owes no one anything on them three acres," he had told her.

236 Joe Cobb Crawford

Two hours later, in the Blue Ridge law offices of Edwards and Shaw, Lee received a notarized Warranty Deed. By the end of the day, she would be recorded as the legal owner of her dream property. Edwards and Shaw would collect five hundred dollars in legal fees. Foster Realty would have sixty-thousand dollars electronically credited to their bank account.

It would be hers unless within three days she decided to rescind and terminate the deal. That was not going to happen. Buying the plot was certain in Lee's otherwise jumbled mind. She had already scheduled a well to be drilled on the site on the next day.

She had fallen in love with the property on her second visit. Unbeknownst to anyone, she had returned to the place a week before informing Mr. Foster she would buy it. While there she secretly stepped off exactly where her cabin would go—situated on a knoll with a mountain in the background. The front porch would overlook the meadow where the creek peacefully meandered. *This is where I will spend my Golden Years,* she kept telling herself. *At sunset from my rocking chair I'll look across the meadow and rest my eyes on a mountain.* Her long awaited dream was finally coming true.

Lee was there early the next morning, an hour

before the drillers arrived.

As she drove up, she looked at the knoll and again imagined her cabin sitting there. Where to locate the well would not be critical. Underground aquifers ran everywhere under the area, or so the drilling company owner had told her.

When they arrived and were shown the property lines' location, she left them to their work. She traveled to the courthouse in Blue Ridge, where she submitted her plans and building permit form. She also informed the local utility co-op that she needed electrical service.

Around noon, she returned to see felled shrubs and saplings surrounding a ten by ten gouged out clearing. A red dirt pile encircled a shallow pit. Lee heard only the burble of the creek. The company's drilling rig was idle, parked nowhere near the clearing. In clusters, the workers distanced themselves from the pit, some smoking cigarettes. Two new guys had joined the work crew—the company's owner and a non-crew member. He looked familiar, maybe a curious native of the area.

Blowing smoke over his shoulder, one worker paced in a circle. Another sneered at the dugout clearing. Lee approached them and asked, "Is something wrong? Why hasn't the drilling started?"

The owner spoke up. "Miz Cornwell, we have a problem. We really do have a problem here. Dang, this doesn't look good at all." Glancing toward the clearing he twisted his lips and shook his head. He gave a sidelong look at Lee, then at the stranger, and finally gave a frazzled gaze toward the red wet pit.

Lee had seen this strained-eye look before. In law enforcement, that look was prescient. Like an ugly twin, it went nowhere alone—tagging with it was something equally or more ugly. It was usually just as the owner had stated—"a real problem." Not for the faint of heart. She didn't hesitate. "Tell me. What's the problem?"

"Well ..., well, you see Miz Cornwell?" He paused and directed an aching stare at Lee, and then bullet-fast he continued. "You see there in that hole? There's uh ..., there's gold in that hole."

"Really? Gold you say?" Giddy, but doubtful, she rapidly fired the question. Then she snickered and clammed up. A high flying scout crow flew over cawing. Lee looked skyward, hesitated, and then said in a serious tone, "How can you be certain it's gold?"

Not waiting for an answer, she dashed over closer to the edge of the dugout pit. Peering in, she immediately saw something glittering under the midday sun. But it was not a miner's gold nugget. It was a gold tooth, accompanied by several other red-clay-tinctured teeth.

Couched in a mostly decayed skull, they rested peacefully. Strangely different and distinct, but with something amiss—like hatched eggs in a bird's nest or an empty baby shoe. Lee gasped and then stepped back. Biting her fist, she looked into the bright sun and deeply inhaled. She wondered, *Is this happening?*

Out of habit, her law enforcement personage hijacked her restless civilian demeanor. She rushed back to the owner and gave orders, "Okay! Do not move anything! This may be a crime scene. Keep your men away from that dig. I'll have to contact the sheriff."

She scampered about and ordered the crew to stay away from the pit. She reached for her iPhone, but then cussed, "Oh, damn it, this iPhone doesn't work down here!"

She turned and yelled over to the company owner, "I see you have an antennae mounted on that drilling rig. I need to use your CB to contact the sheriff. You okay with that?"

"No problem, Miz Cornwell. Do whatever you got to do. Would you like for me to go get the sheriff and bring him down here for you?"

"No. You stay with your men for now." She and the owner paced toward his drilling rig and the CB radio.

Seeing them march away, the stranger stuck his hands in his pockets and sneaked closer to the pit. He bent his knees, staying low to the ground and out of sight. He saw for the first time what they all had seen. He tilted his head and studied the teeth. In a moment he mumbled, "Oh dear God! It can't be, but it is. That's Homer!"

He feebly stood, placed both hands on his head, and sucked in a deep breath.

Lee now saw his movement and position. She yelled, "Hey! You! Get away from that pit! Nobody go near it!"

Stunned by what he'd seen and deaf to her order, he stumbled backwards a few steps. He leaned forward and his hands went to his knees. Bent over, his ashen face raised and he angled his head toward the meadow. Down Mill Creek, his haunted eyes hunted.

———————

Chapter 26 - OH, THAT THAT EARTH

He waddled from his patrol cruiser up toward the gouged-out red clay hole. Near the site, Lee stood shut-mouthed with the drilling company's crew. Faces downward, they puffed cigarettes and muttered amongst themselves. None looked toward the dig site. It was an unwanted orphan—uglier than sin on Sunday.

Sheriff Darby, an average height, flabby man, wore black khakis. His gut folded over his heavy laden duty belt and his pants were two sizes smaller than a comfortable fit. His milky eyes told Lee that, like her, he too had seen more of the sordid side of mankind than he'd ever wanted to.

Removing a note pad from the pocket of his button stressed white shirt, he began, "Morning folks. Are one of you the owner of this property?" He gave a goat-eyed stare at the drilling company owner. His eyes avoided the obvious dig site. Lee said nothing. Hands held behind her back, and with head bowed she rolled each ankle, pretending to examine her muddy shoes. The sheriff's question caused her to think, *Technically, I could get out of owning this mess. I could rescind ownership. It's only one day into the three day rescinding period.*

"Uh. No sir. I'm not the owner," said the drilling company owner. We're just here to drill a well for this lady, Miz Cornwell." He removed his cap and pointed it toward Lee.

Lee wondered if she'd unconsciously exposed her expertise when the discovery was made or maybe when she called the sheriff. Being the go-to person on a physical evidence search had never been on her retirement wish list. A regular civilian was what she had wanted to be—blissfully ignorant, acceptably complacent, and responsible for nothing pertaining to law enforcement matters. Her retirement mantra would be: *Hear no evil; see no evil. Not my circus; not my monkey.*

Sheriff Darby turned toward Lee and slapped his notebook against his left palm. He asked, "Miz Cornwell, are you the person who spoke with our dispatcher?"

"Yes sir, I reported the find."

"Are you the owner of the property where...where the "find" was discovered?"

She paused before answering, her mind and

memory both numb from the sudden reality overload. Hearing the creek gurgle returned her awareness. She gathered her scrambled thoughts. She hadn't considered for even a nanosecond since making the purchase that she would not to be its owner. Now, like a ghost from the past, the notion swept in. In her logical, but confounded mind she thought, *I could go to my attorney and have him cancel my purchase. I could do that.* Her sentimental dream echoed louder in rage. *It's mine! I saved for years for this land and it's mine. Besides, this may be nothing more than the body of a long ago mountain settler. Maybe that's all it is.*

Sheriff Darby crinkled his brow, mustered a pirate's smile, and repeated, "Miz Cornwell. You are the owner. Is that correct?"

"Yes, oh yes. I just bought the land yesterday. It's mine."

Flipping open his notebook he continued, "What is your full name, Miz Cornwell?"

"Lee Ellen Bandy Cornwell," she muttered, struggling to concentrate. Intrusive requests and images from the past competed and collided in her floundering mind. She asked herself, *What's going on here? Why is he asking me questions? That's my job. I ask the questions.* She had forgotten for the moment that she no longer worked in law enforcement.

"Do you have a husband Miz Cornwell? If so, what is his name and where can he be reached?

"No. No, I'm single." Lee bit her lip. She brushed back her hair, looked away, and counted: one Mississippi, two Mississippi ...then continued, "Many years ago I was married, but not now."

"Oh, I see. Well, Miz Cornwell, I'll have several other questions to ask you later, but for now the main question I have for you is this, "Do you have any problem signing a consent-to-search form? If there are human remains, as you told our dispatcher, then we'll need to bring Detective Jones down here to do an investigation. You okay with us looking around?"

"Sure. No problem. Do whatever your procedures call for."

"Good. Very good. Let's have a look at the remains. Can you show me where they are located?"

Lee turned and less energetically pointed in the direction of the teeth. "Over there in that dug out hole. The drillers were only getting ready to drill—clearing out some..."

Sheriff Darby took slow measured steps toward

the dig, this time slapping the notebook against his upper thigh with each step. Lee stayed put. She'd seen enough.

Soon he returned and told Lee, "We'll need to get Jones out here to take a closer look. I'll radio the dispatcher and get him on the way. So, please don't go anywhere. He'll have questions for both you and the well drillers. You okay with that?"

"Sure. Sure. No problem. I'm here for ..."

"Okay, he said, giving Lee a suspicious glance."

He strolled back to his cruiser and opened its door. He flopped down, keyed in the station dispatcher, and made his requests. Lee tuned out the amplified coded messages. She'd heard them all too often. She bent her tired eyes across the meadow, across the creek, to a cabin. There sat the stranger—maybe her future neighbor—his eyes fixed on the cruiser as he rocked on the front porch. She watched him soak up the local protect and serve routine.

———————

"Sheriff, the State boys will need to be brought in. I don't want to risk tainting this scene," said Detective Jones. He held two large labeled plastic bags. In each

246 Joe Cobb Crawford

was a soil sample from the dig area. Standing at his side was an attentive young officer. His shoulders were stiff and he had cop's eyes—void of expression. "Trooper Burnett" was penned over his left pectoral. He held an electronic touchpad and a camera.

"You really think there's been a crime committed here, Detective Jones? What makes you think that? Hell! That body's bound to have been buried for over forty years. Nothing left to identify but a few old rotten teeth."

"That's it exactly, Sheriff. There's nothing there. Never was anything there, but the skull. We're missing the body that goes with that skull and that gold tooth." Holding up the plastic bags he said, "We'll sieve through these soil samples back at the lab, but I'm ninety-nine percent certain no other bone fragments will be found."

Sheriff Darby was stunned. He puckered his face at the plastic bags, then wiped sweat from his brow and bristled, "Mad-cat-almighty! This beats all I ever seen! Just when I thought I'd seen it all, a Turdinator Wagon wrecks in my county." He shook his head and continued, "I guess I'd better notify the 'Staties' and start searching the Tri-state missing person's reports from half a hundred years ago."

He ambled back toward his cruiser. Suddenly

he stopped, looked back, and issued an order to the trooper: "Get the crime scene tape and encircle that dig. Take those folks down to the creek and have them stay there. You stay and secure the ..."

Detective Jones interrupted the sheriff's order: "Hold off on taping the area, Sheriff. But *do* get those people away from the site. Keep them away. It's not safe for anyone to be up there."

The sheriff snapped loose the release on his Smith and Wesson 45. With his right hand on the handle, his pale eyes scanned. Staring at the cleared site, he shouted back to Detective Jones, "Explain, please!"

"It's to the left of that dig about fifty feet— behind that outcropping of rocks. Hard to see it for the undergrowth. Hole in the ground with a steel plate covering it. May be nothing but an abandoned well or spring. Maybe it's an old 1800s mineshaft. Copper veins ran all under this property! It could be just a sink hole, but it's not safe up there. Keep everyone away from that place."

———————

Chapter 27 - ALL'S WELL THAT ENDS WELL DIGGING

Lee wandered the creek side, skipped rocks, and tried to forget about the dig site. The rushing waters were a great diversion—they took her mind off the situation. At the waters' edge, like shirtless Indians, the drilling crew gathered. They sat cross-legged on the green grass having a powwow, eating their sack lunches.

Sheriff Darby walked over officiously slapping his notebook on his thigh as Lee drew near the drilling crew. He yanked up his sagging pants, straightened his duty belt, and then cleared his throat.

Pointing over his right shoulder with his thumb he gave notice, "Well, folks, sorry to rain on y'all's parade, but ain't goin' to be no well drilled up there for a few days. What we got is a real mess. May even be a crime scene. So, don't any of y'all go back up there."

"You mean I can't even go get my chainsaw, axes, and shovels we left up there?" squawked the drilling company owner.

"'At's right. You'll be arrested if you do. I hate it,

but I got to follow the letter of the law on this. Detective Jones found some stuff up there that needs seen about and can't nobody go diddling with the evidence. Law says I got to get the Georgia Bureau of Investigation in here to figure this out."

Lee recognized the pattern and knew the imminent procedure. Last time it was at Grant Park. She had to stand down and turn the case over to the GBI. A dead body had been found. The jurisdiction flipped and she had to bow out.

She ambled up to the sheriff and asked, "Sheriff, anything more you need from me?"

"No, Miz Cornwell." He opened his note book and reviewed his report. "We have your contact info. Is this cell-phone number the best way to reach you?"

"That'll reach me. Am I good to go now?"

"You're free as a bee, Miz Cornewll. We'll be in touch."

———————

Lee drove her Bronco back to Morganton Point Campground near Blue Ridge. Before opening her door, she noticed a stray dog lying under her trailer.

He yapped once, looked indignant, like his property had been trespassed, but then stuck his tail between his legs and left. The dog captured her attention since she had been a K-9 unit detective. She stepped outside and watched the dog lope down the gravel road.

Just before she dropped into a lawn chair her iPhone vibrated. *Maybe that's the sheriff. Maybe they know something new. No. It's too soon. The GBI does nothing fast.*

"Hello, this is officer ..." She caught her mistake and correctly identified herself. "Yes, this is Lee Cornwell speaking."

"Uh. Miz Cornwell? This is Donnie Griggs out here at the co-op. I was calling you to tell you about the electric service you wanted installed down there on that creek. Is this a good time to talk?"

"Oh. Sure, Donnie."

Guess I'd better tell him to hold off on installing electric service for now.

"Well, Miz Cornwell, I wanted to tell you about the cost to put electric service into that place. It won't be just a tap and a transformer we'd need to install to get power to your place. It won't be cheap. There's no power lines within a half mile. We're going to haf' ta set a bunch of poles and run a new, seventy-two hundred volt line down there. That's even before we can begin to install your cabin's low voltage service. You see what I'm saying?"

"Well, yes, I do mostly, but I have a question. Why a new line? There's a cabin across the creek. Where is it getting its power from?"

"You mean Jeff's cabin?"

"I guess. Don't know. Didn't meet the cabin's owner."

"Well, he gens his own electricity. Leastwise I know he don't buy any power from the co-op. He's what they call 'off the grid.' I think he has solar cells and batteries."

"Really? Makes his own electricity, huh?" Lee faked fascination.

"Yep, he was doing it even before it was cool to do so. He's an electrician, ya know? You may want to talk to him about installing your low voltage service lateral once we get the new high voltage line installed. Maybe he'll give you a discount, since y'all are going to be neighbors."

"Mr. Griggs, some things have changed. There is going to be a delay before I need electrical service. Please hold up until I call you back. It'll be a few days."

"Well, that's okay. But now you may want to think again about that solar power. That stuff's expensive to install, expensive to maintain, and don't work so well on cloudy days. Guess I maybe should not have told you about your neighbor's electric power."

"No. That's not the hold up. Some issues have come up that will have to be settled before I'll need electrical service. So please place my order on hold until I call you back."

"No problem. Just give us a call when you're ready."

———————

The conversation with Donnie Griggs roused Lee's curiosity, but not about solar power. She didn't know a kilo-watt from a killed canary. But, this guy across the creek, the electrician, was a different bird. Her muddled mind rambled. *He'd surely place high on a GBI's 'person of interest' list. Uninvited he showed up at the dig site, he snooped around like a cat, but rabbited out before the sheriff's men questioned him.*

Lee thought about going back to Mill Creek. Busy and distracted, she'd forgotten to shop for food. A little out-of-the-way grocery store was on the road there. *While in the area I could shop and visit with my maybe eventual neighbor. I could ask him why he didn't stick around earlier today. More importantly, I'll find out why he looks familiar. Nothing going to happen until the GBI team gets here, anyway.* She jumped in her Bronco, cranked it, and sped out toward her property.

———————

Chapter 28 - LOVE ALL, TRUST A FEW

Lee geared down her Bronco and splashed into the first branch on Old Epworth Road. At midstream she stopped, cut the engine, and lingered in the surroundings. She heard water splatter on mossy rocks. Downstream, she saw a waterfall lined with emerald mountain laurels. Deeply she inhaled their scent—clean, fresh, and pungent. Her mind was at rest, her soul was soothed, and calmness ruled. Far from the day's tumult she escaped. Mill Creek lay ahead about a half mile.

Driving on, she reached a fork in the graveled road. To the left, the Old Epworth Road continued and crossed Mill Creek, where this cabin was located. To her right, the road led up to her place. Going there was now not possible. A strung-up crime scene tape across the road prevented entry. Forced left, she crossed the creek, and soon saw a dirt road she hoped would lead to the cabin.

A purple haze sunset grabbed her attention, but then a loud chaotic blare alarmed her and made her flinch. The sound was like that of nineteen cracked clarinets played by the deaf. The noise spilled down the mountain and reverberated through the meadow.

At the mountain's top she saw the ensemble—a flock of guineas flying over. Like Huey helicopters, these gray fowls speckled with small white dots and crimson heads, came in for a joint landing. They took roost on a loblolly's top limbs. This lone pine sat near the base of the mountain at the entrance to a hollow. Again she stopped the Bronco, taking in the colorful celebration of the day's end.

The cabin came into view and Jeff sat there in a rocker on the front porch. Alongside him a long-eared blue tick hound rested. Seeing Lee approach, the dog leaped from the porch and charged the vehicle. Enshrouded in a cloud of dust, he barked fiercely at the creeping black tires. When the Bronco slowed, the hound muscled up, stood rock hard, and the stiff hair on his neck spiked. He yelped intermittently between showing his teeth, growling disapproval, and snarling at the tires. Lee parked, shut off the engine, but stayed inside the Bronco.

Jeff removed a toothpick clenched between his teeth. He held one hand over his forehead and rose. Supporting his lower back with his other hand, he yelled, "Hello. Can I help you?" He then scolded the hound, "Shut your mouth Blue! Behave yourself. Get back up here on this porch."

The dog obeyed. Begrudgingly, he looked at the Bronco while he trotted back. He leaped onto the porch. With his head between his front paws, he hung out his tongue about a foot and panted. Like a metronome, he drummed a beat with his tail on the porch planks.

Lee got out of her vehicle, assessing the cabin. She showed no fear, but kept one eye on the dog and one on the porch steps. She felt for her can of mace clasped to the duty belt that she normally wore.

Her K-9 training had taught her to move slowly when confronted by a vicious animal. She'd also learned the difference between a bluff and a real threat from an agitated dog. She'd quickly assessed Blue's performance as worthy of an Oscar.

As she got closer to the porch, Jeff said, "Hi Lee. Come have a seat. Ignore that dog. He's all bark and no bite. He wouldn't hurt a flea."

Looking up and brushing back her hair she asked, "Are you Jeff, the guy that does electrical work? I'm Lee Ellen Cornwell."

Where have I seen this guy? Was it at police academy boot camp? she asked herself.

"Yes, I'm Jeff Cagle, or what's left of him." He pointed to a rocker, smiled and said, "Won't you join us? Ole Blue here and me were about to watch the sun go down."

Scoping the porch, Lee ascended the steps. Hands on hips, she snapped, "How'd you know my name? Have we met before?"

This will out Mr. Mystery Man. But why can't I remember?

"Sure we've met, but it was years ago. Never have forgotten you, Lee."

"You'll have to give me a hint. I'm ... I'm drawing a blank."

"Well, it was at Epworth—Mr. Chastain's eighth grade class. I was the kid one row over from you, sat at the back of the room."

Jeff Cagle—Person of interest? Hardly! He's that kid who always slept through class—him and those losers who passed gas and carved their initials on their desktops.

"Oh yeah, you were that kid who caught chickens at night," she said, straining to scan his arms for scars and needle tracks, but seeing none. "Yeah, it's coming back to me now." She leaned forward, bit her lip, and shook her head. "It's been a while since those *good old days.*"

"So, what brings you back to God's Country? I saw you earlier today across the creek. Guess you saw the tape the sheriff put across the road. Is that your place over there?"

"Yes, it's mine, but now it looks like it will be a few days before I can get on with building a cabin there. That's why I came to see you."

"Oh, darn, I'm disappointed. I thought maybe you'd come to tell me that you were ready to resume our cut-short eighth grade romance." He chuckled while pinching and ruffling Ole Blue's neck.

Lee did not respond. Instead she grimaced at the dog who sprang up to bite at a lightning bug that glided by.

Jeff had embarrassed himself, maybe Lee, too. His cavalier comment had left him vulnerable and created an awkward moment. He attempted to redeem himself and reset the mood by moving on.

"So, why did you come to see me, Lee?"

"Understand you do electrical work.   Is that correct?"

"Well, I do some work.   Not all I get asked to do, but I do take on a few projects to beat the boredom.   Whatcha' got?"

"Need something called an 'electrical service installation.'   Well, let me qualify that.   I'll need it when they take down that crime scene tape."

"Yeah, I could do that, but you *do* know the cost will be higher than Big Frog Mountain?   If you haven't noticed, no utility lines have ever been run down here to Mill Creek."

"Yes, I missed that, but Donnie at the co-op briefed me on it."

The sun silhouetted the indigo mountains.   Only a faint violet shade of light remained.   A whippoorwill began its lonely cry.   All of a sudden, soft and sincere he asked, "So, where did you go?   I mean, where have you been all these years, Lee?   You went away our freshman year.   I remember it like it was yesterday."

Lee clammed up, not wanting to explain the drubbing that fate had put on her youthful aspirations.   She defaulted to her comfortable *Dragnet* cop demeanor—Miz Joe Friday. Hesitating to answer, she flashed a congenial smile.

"That's a long story. More drama than you'd probably care to hear. So, tell me about 'Jeff the Chicken Catcher.' You still catch chickens?" Then she snickered.

"No! Let me be clear about that ... Hell, No!" Then he grinned and winked at Lee and went on to say, "Haven't caught chickens since high school. Fact is, catching chickens dang-near stopped me from graduating—worked too much. But, Old Blinky Blair dealt me a deuce. Gave me half a point to pass me in Senior English."

Lee sensed that, like her, he didn't want to roll out his life's failures. Silence returned and night fell. Each retreated to their comfort zone. Crickets chirped and the frogs continued croaking their message in the meadow. Breaking the silence, she asked, "So, did you stay or move away after you graduated?"

"I moved on, but didn't follow the herd. They went to Atlanta. I got a job in Charlotte. Started night school and studied electronics. Then Vietnam came along. It got me focused on studying, staying out of the draft, and staying alive. Got an engineering degree. I worked for several large corporations over the years. Finally, after enjoying all I could stand of corporate life, I jumped ship—moved back here right after 9/11. Funny isn't it? Half a hundred years gone and here I sit—right back where I started. Watching Mill Creek roll on. Hey, looks like you too have come home to roost in the mountains."

Looking straight ahead, Jeff flexed his hands, studied them, then turned to her and asked, "So what brings you back, Lee? What have you been doing all these years?"

"Oh a little of this; a little of that. Like you, I got tired of the big city insanity. Took early retirement and pulled up stakes. Now, I'm planning on becoming a recluse, here in the mountains." Again deflecting the topic, she asked, "Tell me, Jeff. I understand you are totally off the grid. Don't use the co-op's electricity. How's that working out for you?"

"For me it's working great. For others, I do not recommend it."

"Oh. And why's that?"

"It's not a one-size-fits-all, silver bullet energy solution."

"What do you mean? It prevents paying high electric bills, doesn't it?"

"Oh, sure. The co-op gets no monthly jingle from me. But here is the thing most people don't get about solar-electric energy, it's overall cost is high when you figure in everything. Things like the cost to buy and install hardware and the cost to repair it.

"So, you're telling me solar power for my cabin's not a good thing?"

"Well, no. Just sayin' all things should be considered first. House roofs everywhere now are covered with those black solar cells. Their owners brag, 'Hey I'm protecting planet earth. Hey, I'm stopping global warming, saving money and looking out for my children.' But they don't consider that processing silica, the element used to make solar cells, is a carcinogenic process. People mining and processing the silica—mostly Chinese—die from either cancer or silicosis. Those black roof owners tell themselves they are good guys, when they're in fact contributing to the death of people."

Jeff pointed out from the porch to Mill Creek and said, "See that creek? Looking back, I wish I had installed a Geo-Thermal system. That water is a constant source for BTUs. It could save money, save energy, and help save the planet."

"I'm not sure some parts of the planet are worth saving," muttered Lee with a tight-lipped smile. "Especially some parts of Atlanta. And what on earth is a B-T-U?"

They both smiled.

"Guess I'm boring you with all the techno-babble."

"No. Not really. It's sort of interesting. I'm just not … tech-savvy."

The cool breeze and sounds from the meadow had relaxed Lee. The odd harmony of the croaking frogs, crickets and the cicadas combined with Mill Creek's burbling had taken her mind off the day's worries.

Suddenly, something on the creek bank cracked. Lee reached for her duty belt. *No belt! No Glock 45! Get low!* She rushed to the porch's edge and scanned the meadow, looking for movement. She saw only darkness and an occasional lightning bug flicker.

She relaxed when she saw her parked Bronco. A deep breath led her to think. *Did he see me reach for my Glock? Guess he thinks I'm a nut case, now. Why did I do that?*

Easing down the steps, she turned, and said, "Jeff, I gotta go." His eyes traced her carefully placed steps toward her vehicle.

Into the dark he awkwardly cried out, "Lee, I'm fixing some trout tomorrow evening. Also, having some stuff from my garden. Come back around dark-thirty. Ole Blue and I hope you'll join us for supper."

Lee did not respond. He listened to her footsteps on the gravel road. A minute later, as though she'd just heard his words, she replied, "Alright. See you tomorrow evening."

Ole Blue had trailed alongside Lee, safely escorting her back to the Bronco. While she entered and slammed the door, he cocked his hind leg and marked the passenger side's front tire. She cranked up and drove away, back to her camper.

———————

Chapter 29 - A DYING BUSINESS

Bruce Foster prided himself on being "in-the-know." With his office scanner and his Jeep's CB, he kept in the loop on Fannin County happenings. He'd heard Lee call the Sheriff's office and wasted no time contacting a former business associate:

"Conyers Crematory and Funeral Home. May I help you please?"

"Yes ma'am, how you doing? Could you put me through to Mr. Conyers, please?

"Why, certainly. Just one second."

"This is Sylvester Conyers. With whom do I have the pleasure of speaking?

"Syl? Oh. Hey Syl. This is Bruce Foster, in Blue Ridge. Friend, we have a little problem up here."

"What kind of problem?"

"Well, it's nothing insurmountable for a man with your charm and influence. But it's something you need to see about and soon. Got a Sheriff up here snooping around."

"Snooping? For what?"

"Cadavers! I'm talking about those cadavers we took care of for you a while back when your incinerator went south."

"Well, hell! They're dead. What kind of problem can they be causing? You *did* take care of them properly as we discussed, didn't you? Damn it Bruce! I paid you good money to take care of those cadavers! Eight thousand dollars if memory serves me right."

"Chill Syl, it's no big thing. Just a little tidying up needed. That's all. Everything's cool.

"Well, what's your concern then? Why'd you call me?"

"Here's the deal. Since 9/11, real estate business's been slow as a snail race. I needed money bad. Didn't really want to, but the other day I sold my property that borders the place where we dropped those cadavers. Lady from Atlanta wouldn't have anything *but* that property. She offered me more money than I could turn down. Darn if her well digger didn't uproot some dead remains on that plot. No way was it one of those bodies we dropped in that sinkhole. Those cadavers are long gone. They're a thousand feet down in water. Read it myself with my sonar. No way did one float back up."

"So how did the body get to the surface?"

"That's what I'm telling you Syl. It's a body someone else put there. Not one of your cadavers." He continued, "There's no risk as long as the GBI stays off the property. If they come in, they'll camp out and look under every rock. I don't want that. You don't want that. Here's what I'm asking you to do. Since you're related to the Georgia Speaker of the House, I think you can easily do this. Give him a call. Ask him to put the brakes on sending the GBI up here. Tell him tourism and business in Fannin County will take another beating if the GBI and the Atlanta news start hanging around. I'm telling you, Syl, if they show up, my real estate business will tank. Understand what I'm saying?"

"Yeah, I got the picture, but a question for you. Are you certain about this?"

"Got it straight from the horse's mouth. Caught the scoop on my CB monitor. The lady radioed in a dead body find to Sheriff Darby. Syl, I know for a fact that body ain't your cadaver, but it don't matter, you see? Later, I heard the Sheriff's dispatcher send a detective out to gather evidence. It's solid, Syl. We can't delay on this. Hear what I' m saying? You and me won't look good in those orange jump suits."

"I'll handle it. Don't forget my phone number."

———————

"Trooper Burnett, I need for you to use your computer wizardry to help the fine folks of Fannin County," said Sheriff Darby as he stepped into Burnett's office.

"Sure Sheriff Darby. Be glad to. What do you need me to do?"

"Need you to find out who this Miz Cornwell *really* is. I don't like her. Somethin' 'bout her's a half bubble off level. Don't like the way she talks—too polite, uses fancy law officer words."

Tearing the pink copy from his notepad, he handed it to Trooper Burnett and continued, "Enter the report in the system first. Then give it to the dispatcher to file away. Then take that tag number I copied and see who it's registered to. Don't stop until you got this possum treed. Hear me youngster?"

Smiling broadly he said, "Yes, sir. I'm on it Sheriff Darby."

"Detective Jones," Sheriff yelled. "Dag-nab-it Jones! Where'd you go?" Jones had taken a seat in his backroom office, near the jail cells. The two bags of teeth, decayed skull, and dirt lay atop his desk.

Thumbs up and index fingers pointing like six-shooters at the evidence, the sheriff approached Jones. "Put that stuff away. We ain't got time to divine old bones and teeth."

"Sure Sheriff. I'll get it done. Want me to get a heads-up to the district GBI office?"

"Nope. I'll call them when ... when and if I think we need 'em. Gonna let the cream rise to the top before we go churning the butter on this case. Got my meaning Detective Jones?"

"Oh, sure. I'll just secure the evidence for now."

Tapping his belly with both hands, Sheriff Darby announced, "Well boys. My supper's getting cold. Think I'll get on home before Louise throws it out to the dogs. See y'all in the morning."

———————

Chapter 30 - SKY CRY

Why does the sky cry
for what might have been?
Can a petal, dry
Bloom with life again?

Tears' mission was to seek
Petals dry to find
Splash, dash, atop the creek
Rain and fate danced blind.

———————

The sky was steely gray the next morning. Lee stayed in her camper, sleeping until after ten. Chattering kids bustled by, going to swim before the rain came. They awakened her. By force of habit she lunged for her Glock.

Rubbing her eyes, she stumbled to the tiny kitchenette's cupboard. All she saw inside was a coffee sack and half a pop tart. Biting the tasteless dry treat she mused,

Darn, I still haven't shopped. Can't even remember

where I was yesterday. You're losing it kiddo.

She made a pot of coffee, hoping to clear the cobwebs. Then recalling her visit with the electrician, she reached for her phone to check for missed calls. None. After two stout cups of coffee, she asked herself,

Did the Sheriff tell me to come by his office today? No, he said he would be back in touch with me. Maybe he tried and the phone doesn't work here. And that guy, my eighth grade classmate, what did I tell him? I like Ole Blue. Yeah, I did tell him I'd join him for dinner tonight. Why did I do that? Nincompoop!

———————

Early evening was same as the morning, only gloomier—gray, overcast, languid air, with the feel of a dentist's office. The feel changed when Lee again brought the Bronco to a stop midstream of the creek. As the day before, the sounds, the smells, and the wet green sights transported her far from her worries.

Out of nowhere the questions came—*"what was the best day and the worst day of your life?"* It was her favorite scene from the movie *City Slickers*. Quickly her trained mind compartmentalized, *Not going there; too much touchy-feely to handle just yet. I got to stay on task.*

Another question rushed in:

So, what would my life have been like had I come home earlier? What if I'd returned after I got my Horticulture degree? Or, what if I'd bailed when I graduated the police academy? Could I have made it here? Pace sure is slower. Better environment to raise my son. Fannin County and Atlanta both have crime and shrubbery, no doubt. Someone keeps them in line. Could have been me. Maybe.

Driving on a half mile, she saw the crime scene tape. It was still up, but was twisted and had drooped. It looked brighter under the gray sky. She made a left and on to Jeff's cabin.

Like a palace guard, Ole Blue bounced from the porch barking. Quickly seeing and smelling the Bronco's black tires, he returned to his post. No barbarians to defend against a castle siege this evening.

Jeff sat in a swing. He rose, smiled, and said, "Hey Lee! Glad to see you back. Hope you brought your appetite with you. Supper's on, soon as potatoes finish baking. Did you have a good day?"

"Well, yes, but very uneventful. Caught up on my ZZZ's and reading. No word from the sheriff on my place across the creek, either. See any traffic over there today?"

"No, but I was gone this morning. They had a power outage at the Piggly Wiggly while I was there. Car hit a power pole. Co-op got the power back on, but the surge damaged their refrigeration unit. Helped them find the problem." Jeff cut a smile at Lee and continued, "Got steaks for my services, all tax free barter. So, the menu's changed tonight. How do you like your rib-eye cooked?"

"Like mine medium-well. Got another glass of that red wine you're drinking?"

"Oh, sorry. What was I thinking? Be right back. Keep Ole Blue company. He likes wine too, but I have to watch him. I think he's Irish. Don't know when he's had enough."

Ole Blue, hearing his name, arose, shook himself, and followed Jeff to the cabin's screen door. Jeff gave him a pat on the head and playfully pulled at his long right ear. Ole Blue gave a fake nip at his hand and turned and lay back down.

Handing the wine glass to Lee, who had now settled in a rocking chair, he said, "about ten minutes till tater time. Are you hungry?"

"I sure am." She didn't tell him that half a pop tart was all she'd eaten all day. Nor did she reveal her long ago weight and eating struggles.

Supper was a quiet affair, accompanied by mostly Jeff's small talk. He shared some of the problems he'd had when he built his cabin. Questions from the past, personal demons, and yesterday's regrets weren't discussed. He appeared content to have a companion to dine with other than his dog.

After supper they returned to the porch. A soft slow drizzle hung in the meadow. The creek flowed and tumbled noisily—no night critters covered its sound. Later, a steady rain came. Both sat silent, sharing the secure solitude of drops tapping the porch's tin roof.

———————

Chapter 31 - TROUBLE AT THE HOGLY WOGLY

The Fannin County Sheriff's Department was swamped. Even before Trooper Burnett scraped the black from his toast, an ugly day had begun. Ironically, a full moon—the usual suspect of fomenting unrest—was not the cause.

At four A.M. he'd arrested a married couple. Liquor was involved. What started as a disturbing the peace call, resulted in both parties being arrested—one for domestic violence and the other for obstructing an officer. They'd shown contempt for Trooper Burnett, each other, and anyone else who crossed their vengeful path. Cuffed and stuffed in the cruiser's back seat, he'd had to stop, separate them, and shackle their kicking legs before getting them to jail.

Later, a loose horse had wandered to greener grass near a highway edge. Sheriff Darby apprehended, haltered, and tied the wayward equine to a maple tree. From the sheriff's clear description of the horse, the dispatcher recognized its rightful owner, called her, and the owner retrieved the runaway.

The department's manpower was stressed further by a vehicle accident. The collision and power outage that scored rib-eye steaks for Jeff and Lee from the Piggly-Wiggly, created a full morning for the Sheriff's department.   An E911 dispatch triggered Sheriff Darby's and Trooper Burnett's second call before the dew dried on the apples at Mercier's Orchard.

"Base to Unit 02, do you read me?"

"Copy, loud and clear. What you got?"

"Traffic snarl at the Hogly-Wogly. Single car clipped a power pole. Need you there pronto. Copy?"

"Piggly-Wiggly, confirm?"

"Affirmative. Sheriff Darby en route from base. Copy?"

"Copy, I'm on my way."

Blue lights gyrating, headlights flashing and sirens blaring, Trooper Burnett arrived to find two separate wrecks and the woods on fire. He quickly began securing the area and kept loitering spectators away from the smoke-clouded three ring circus. The arcing power lines had sparked and ignited leaves. A rubbernecker, slowing to check out the fireworks, had been rear-ended. Traffic stopped in both directions as siren wails from an EMS van and a fire truck grew louder.

Soon the highway patrolmen and the news media arrived. Sheriff Darby met with everyone. Trooper Burnett assisted in directing and detouring traffic around the accidents. With traffic flow back to normal, around noon they both returned to the Sheriff's Office where Sheriff Darby filed reports with the dispatcher's help.

Trooper Burnett munched fast on a sandwich while drilling down into the Georgia Law Enforcement Vehicle data base. His eyes popped wide open when he read under the header, *Lee Ellen Cornwell, Occupation: Law Enforcement Detective, Fulton County Police Department.* Spewing sweet tea from his mouth, he jumped to his feet and raced to Sheriff Darby, who was chatting with the dispatcher.

"Sheriff, you aren't going to believe this! That tag number you gave me is registered to one of us. I mean the car belongs to a law enforcement officer."

"What? You can't be serious! Did you look for it on the criminal hotlist?"

"No Sheriff. The computer says it's not hot. It's registered to Lee Ellen Cornwell, a law enforcement officer in Fulton County."

"Hogwash! That computer's dumber than a

bucket of rocks! But, come to think of it, she did talk like an officer. I'll call my old buddy, Darrel Davis, down there in Atlanta. He owes me a back scratch. See if *he* knows her. Thank ye, Trooper Burnett. You do good work."

The black and white Atlanta cruiser pulled to the curb and flashed its blue dome lights. A slim built, stiff shouldered pedestrian strolled up and gazed inside. He wore a canary golfer's hat, a buttoned suit coat with no tie, and a pair of shabby shoes that screamed "sore feet."

"Hawkins, you look 'bout as natural out of prison and on the street, as a pregnant nun," said Officer Welch, half-smiling.

"Good to see you, too. How's your wife and my children doing?" His skin was jail-time bleached white, and his dark eyes, bright as a snake's, glared defiant scorn.

"Get in Hawkins. Take a ride with me."

"Love to, but I ain't got time. Got an appointment with my parole officer." He pushed back his hat, looked listlessly down the street and continued, "You know what they say, 'ain't got the time, don't mess with crime."

"Hop in. This won't take long. I'll drop you off there, soon as we chat."

"Chat about what? Done talking to the law. Finished when that bitch cop Cornwell did her chattin' with the judge and put me away." He spit on the sidewalk.

"Get in. Some news you might want to know about Officer Cornwell." He winked at him, and shoved open the passenger side door.

Hawkins folded his lanky body into the cruiser, and said "Now I got to be at the P.O. place at two. Can't be late. Got me a one way ticket out of the house and don't want to break back in. Un'stand?"

Officer Welch nodded his head, appeared in deep thought, but said nothing. As the cruiser pulled from the curb, his cold gray eyes stared soberly at the traffic ahead. His stubby hands gripped and twisted the steering wheel, and his expression was as far removed from empathy as birth is removed from murder. After passing through the third red light, he barked

"She's up in Fannin County, Georgia. Holed up in her camper on Blue Ridge Lake. Her pinged phone and GPS placed her at Morganton Point."

Hawkins cut his eyes out his window and ground his teeth. He blinked once, swiveled his head back toward Welch, and said, "So why you think I give a fuck where she's camping?"

"You were getting free room and board at the Greybar Hotel when your mama died. *She* put you there and kept you there. Thought you might want to know where she's chillin'. Now get the hell out! You're stinking up my cruiser."

The cruiser slid to a stop. Hawkins slammed its door. Teeth grinding, his snake eyes tracked the black and white vehicle of justice as it sped out of sight.

———————

Chapter 32 - ACROSS THE CREEK

*W*here is Ole Blue, Jeff wondered as he drove his pickup through the creek crossing and up the dusty road leading to his cabin? *He's always here to meet me. That dog knows me better than anyone and he still likes me,* he mused and chuckled to himself.

The pickup was parked. Ole Blue, wet from the tip of his nose to the tip of his tail, came in a gallop from the meadow. He stopped short of getting to Jeff who had just slammed the truck door. He half-yelped and growled one time. He then turned and ran back across the meadow toward Mill Creek and then went out of sight.

Jeff pondered. *What has gotten into him? Has he caught another musk rat or a beaver? Why is he down in the creek?*

Tired from a long day's work, he slow stepped in the meadow over to where Ole Blue stood. At the edge of the creek the dog wailed and whined. Coming closer Jeff saw what at first seemed surreal—Lee's motionless body on the other side. On the sloped bank, it lay at a jaunty angle downward, head first. The face and left shoulder were partially submerged in the water.

"Lee!   Dear God in Heaven," he screamed as he jumped from the bank into the creek.   Frantically, he fought through the swift current to the other side. As he knelt, holding her cold limp arm to check for a pulse; he saw the bloody arrow.   Instantly, he scanned side to side and his eyes scouted his all too familiar surroundings.   No pulse and no breathing was found. She was dead.

He gently moved her from the water to the bank's grassy edge.   She lay on her side.   Ole Blue barked, but then jumped in the creek and joined Jeff.   Then he ordered Ole Blue, "Stay here.   I'm going to get the Sheriff. Stay here!"

Sheriff Darby arrived first at the crime scene. He immediately radioed Detective Jones to report for duty. The EMS responders arrived next. They checked her vital signs, found none, but did not move the body. Detective Jones arrived accompanied by the coroner. Jones began taking photos and making notes on his electronic pad. The coroner pronounced her dead and Lee's body was taken to the funeral home.   Detective Jones put yellow tape around the crime scene.

Ole Blue stayed at the scene, but Jeff returned to his cabin.   Sitting alone in a porch rocker, as the sun began to creep behind the mountains he leaned forward with his face in his trembling hands. He fought back tears.

Sheriff Darby and Detective Jones soon left the crime scene and crossed the creek. Parking and leaving the cruiser running with the headlights on, they approached Jeff's porch. Jeff did not acknowledge their presence. Sheriff Darby, with one foot on the bottom porch step and one foot on the ground, looked at Jeff and asked, "When did you find the body?"

Holding his hands to his sides, Jeff flinched as though awakened. A puzzled look crossed his face as he said, "I'm sorry. What did you ask me, Sherriff?"

"At what time did you first see the body?"

"When I got in from work. About an hour ago."

"Do you know anything about that arrow? Seen any hunters or target practicing going on down there on the creek?"

"No Sheriff. I've been gone all day. Wired a cabin in Ellijay today." He paused then said, "This is posted private property, Sheriff. Shouldn't be any hunters in here."

"Well, I know that, but sometimes people forget where the boundary lines are, now don't they? One last question, we may have some more questions later.

Did you move the body?"

Jeff's face contorted. He nervously rubbed his forehead with his right hand. The image of Lee's face under water flashed in his mind. He looked away, hesitated, and answered, "Yes, her head was in the water. I pulled her out of the water and ... I put her where y'all found her." He dropped his head and his chin touched his chest.

"Stay close by the next few days. Let us know if you see any suspicious activity down here. Okay?" He turned and walked away.

Head still bowed, he muttered, "Yes, sir."

The sheriff stopped walking and turned around. He gave Jeff a sideways glance, studying his composure. Then he spoke. "Just one more thing. How were you related to Miz Cornwell?"

"She was a long lost friend, Sheriff. We went to grammar school together in the eighth grade at Epworth. She was going to be my neighbor."

"I see. Stay in touch." Sheriff Darby waddled away toward his cruiser, slapping the note pad on his thigh. He stared across the meadow at crime scene number two now on Mill Creek.

Chapter 33 - STRANGE BEDFELLOWS

"Lieutenant Davis speaking."

"Darrell. Darrell, it's Sheriff Darby up in Blue Ridge again. How's the law and order business in Hotlanta today?"

"Oh, hi, Sheriff Darby. Everything's cool here. What's going on in the mountains?"

"Got some bad news. One of our own has fallen. Remember the retired lady officer I called you about a few days ago? Well, she's dead. Physical evidence looks like a hunting accident, but we're still investigating. Killed by a stray hunting arrow or bolt I guess you'd call it. Damn crazy Bambi hunters! Woods are full of them up here."

"Officer Cornwell is dead? Um, really sorry to hear that. Always a bad day when one of our people in blue goes down."

"Yes sir. A bad day ..." Sheriff Darby, hesitated, waited for Lieutenant Davis to comment, but heard silence.

He continued, "Well, I hate being the bearer of bad news. Goes with the job, you know. Body's at Lark Funeral Home in McCaysville, here. No arrangements yet. Thought y'all might have info on her next of kin and maybe a retired officer's protocol ceremony for her. Maybe fellow officers there would want to attend the funeral."

"Yes, for sure some will. Not a line of duty death, but we still have a protocol. I'm sending an email to our watch commander as we speak. He'll coordinate the ceremony. I'll pass on the word at roll call after next of kin have been notified. Thanks for calling, Sheriff Darby."

––––––––––

Lieutenant Davis was in fact grieved by the death notification, but not for the loss of a fellow law enforcement officer. Lee's demise meant he had lost a key witness. Investigator Welch's case was quickly approaching. With Lee gone, Davis's defense was weakened. She would have solidly corroborated Davis's charge against Investigator Welch.

Outing Welch's career pattern of sexual harassment would have determined and turned the case's outcome. Both Davis and Welch knew this well.

Davis also knew Welch's retirement package loss would net his under-funded police department budget a cool quarter of a million dollars. Davis quickly reviewed his strategy for winning the case. A new case defense was needed, but he wanted all the facts before he developed one.

"Sheriff Darby, this is Darrell again, down in Atlanta. I have a question concerning the death of Officer Lee Cornwell. Do you have a few minutes for questions."

"Sure, Darrell. What do you need?"

"Well, could you email me the evidence file for the investigation of Officer Cornwell's death? Save us both some time."

"I can do that. Well, not me, but I have a computer guru here who can make that happen. I'm computer challenged. Where you coming from?"

"Got some suspects that had it in for Miz Cornwell. Made some threats. The mouthy ones don't usually follow through, but got to cover all bases, you see? You say it was most likely a hunting accident and the kill weapon was an arrow. Has an autopsy been

292   Joe Cobb Crawford

performed?"

"No, we don't do autopsies unless family or D.A. requests one. Ain't got that kind of money in our budget like you folks in Hotlanta. And, yes, it was a high dollar arrow, a bolt they call it. Three razorblade broad-head type point. We'll email you a picture of it. Went right through the heart. Pretty sure it was an accident, but the case is still open."

"Right through the heart, huh? Fine, send it on down. That would be great. Also, get an autopsy run. We'll pick up the tab. Sheriff, if you'll do that for me, I'll sing at your next wedding. Seriously, thanks for your help. Be safe up there, and stay out of them woods."

"You got it. I don't hunt."

———————

Hunting accident, my hind leg, Lieutenant Davis mused, as he slammed down the phone. *Darby knows as well as me that landing a clean shot through the heart is nearly impossible, unless taken at short range. And with a bolt? Negative! He trained for marksmanship, same as me before we did our tour in Nam.*

Lieutenant Davis wasted no time. *Find the motive*

and you find the killer, he told himself. *Inspector Welch certainly has motive, but he's got no guts for killing. Maybe he got someone to do it for him.*

Quickly, Lieutenant Davis took the elevator to the basement where surveillance recordings of department cruisers were stored. He asked for and signed out the video files of Inspector Welch's cruiser log for the last two weeks. Late into the night at the station he studied the videos.

The next morning he visited the Atlanta Parole Office, a recorded stop on Welch's travel log. Their video confirmed Welch had been there. Welch had been in contact with an early released self-defense killer, felon Cedric Hawkins. He had connections. He had motive—avenging Officer Lee Ellen Cornwell's locking him away for seven years. Lieutenant Davis brought Hawkins in for questioning.

————————

Chapter 34 - RETURN AND RETRIEVE

Two weeks after the funeral, the soldier again parked the old van with the cracked windshield at Curtis Switch Crossing.   The same plan and timing would be repeated to infiltrate enemy territory once more. *It worked perfectly the first time. No reason it won't work this time,* he assured himself.

Returning to the site would allow him to admire his perfectly executed work.

The funeral confirmed her death, but I need to relive the adventure. I eloquently ridded society of a Godless evil woman. More of society's trash like her should be taken out. They'll thank me later, he gloated.

Deep down, he had a more personal reason for returning. He had misplaced the locket, the one he'd treasured and had carried with him every day for the last seventeen years. He'd looked everywhere but could not find it. It was more than a lucky charm or a rabbit's foot. Without it, he felt naked, alone, and hopeless. He had to have it back, no matter the cost. Just the feel of it and its clicking sound as he snapped it open and shut soothed his tormented soul. Besides, there is no risk now in returning. Everyone in the county believes that idiot sheriff and thinks it was a hunting accident.

When he dipped under the crime scene tape where he had executed the perfect shot with his crossbow, someone awaited his arrival. Someone he never once imagined was there to greet him. Someone he thought to be clueless and incapable of deciphering his brilliant plan.

Sheriff Darby, hiding behind an outcropping of flint rocks, heard the soldier's approach—the undergrowth and huckleberry bushes brushed his camo fatigues. With each step, the swishing grew louder, overriding the thump and hissing of blood in the sheriff's ears. When the soldier came within ten feet of him, Sheriff Darby stepped out from behind it. With his Smith and Wesson pointed at the soldier, he issued an order, "Stop right there. Get on the ground, hands behind your head."

"Hold on Sheriff! What'er you doing? Why you want me on the ground?"

Sheriff Darby's free hand reached in his pocket. He dangled the locket and said, "This what you looking for, Cornwell?"

Mark Cornwell's eyes went wide open. Then they quickly narrowed. He focused not on the Sheriff's gun but the locket. Sheriff Darby looked straight at Cornwell's face as he dangled the locket from its thin silver chain.

He twirled it once, then flipped the locket into his palm and snapped open its cover. With one eye on Cornwell and the other on the picture inside the locket, Sheriff Darby commented, "Nice looking kid. Damn good thing he's not related to you, Cornwell."

"That's my..." Eyes still concentrated on the locket, his words trailed off.

"No. This boy here is no kin to you at all, Cornwell. But, it don't matter, now. You get on the ground like I told you."

"That bitch tell somebody that? She's a liar. Told it to feel less guilty about putting me in the pen. Keeping my only son away from me."

Sheriff Darby glanced again at the picture inside the locket and responded, "No, checked both y'alls DNA. You know, computers are a wonderful thing. They told me this boy is no kin to you. Now, I told you to get on the ground. You going back where you belong."

298   Joe Cobb Crawford

The soldier turned to one side and kneeled. Before going face down he slid the knife from his shirt sleeve to his hand. The sheriff approached slowly. Placing the locket in his shirt pocket, he reached to remove handcuffs from his duty belt. At his back, both heard a distant crackling of leaves getting closer

The sheriff spun his head, stealing a look toward the rustle. Cornwell wasted no time. With a running lunge, he sliced Sheriff Darby's gut. Blood squirted. The sheriff's white shirtfront turned crimson in less than three seconds. Stunned by the burning pain, he hesitated. Haplessly the sheriff missed a shot at Cornwell. They wrestled for the gun and it dropped from the sheriff's hand. Cornwell swung, landing a solid blow to the sheriff's temple. Knocked cold, Darby lay sprawled on the ground. Hot blood trickled from his knife wound to the forest floor, coating pine needles and moss.

Cornwell ran to the sheriff and removed the locket from the sheriff's pocket. He then ran over and snatched up the gun. He heard, but ignored the growling, the snarling rage, the something galloping toward him. Pointed teeth gleaming, Ole Blue leaped and latched on to Cornwell's wrist, clamping down with every ounce of his being, his sharp teeth piercing

Cornwell's flesh and tendons. Suspending the dog in mid-air, Cornwell tried to shake Ole Blue loose, but lost his grasp of the knife. It dropped, landing without a sound. With his free hand, he separated the dog's clinched jaws and he plunged to the turf, landing on his back with a yelp. Cornwell gave him a brutal kick, slamming him backwards. But Ole Blue was no quitter. He shook off the booting and came back after the now fleeing Cornwell.

Fifty feet into his escape, Ole Blue was hot on his trail and gaining ground fast. Quieter than cancer, with no warning, it happened. The earth under Cornwell's fleeting feet was gone. Like a leaf in a creek, he was carried away by the dirt avalanche, shifting and falling into the old mine shaft. Down into the dark hole his grasping arms and frantic legs flailed as his screams faded. Downward he descended, plunging one thousand feet to an unseen watery graveyard to join the unknown cadavers.

Ole Blue made a sliding stop just short of the dirt avalanche. He ran back, turned, and stood as still as a statue. Sniffing the fresh moldy soil, pungent with plant roots, he yelped continuously as though he had two coons up a tree. He then galloped back to the sheriff. He licked the Sheriff Darby's face and nudged him with his nose.

The sheriff soon gained consciousness. Flinching and groaning from his burning gut, he struggled to his feet.   He removed a back-pocket handkerchief, placed it over bleeding wound, and willed his way back to behind the large flint rock.   There he retrieved his turned-off CB radio and called for help.

———————

EPILOGUE

Sheriff Darby's call for help was promptly responded to by young Trooper Burnett. He came alone and took the sheriff to Fannin Regional Hospital. In two weeks the stitches were removed. He didn't ask what had taken place, but Sheriff Darby—always good with a story—concocted a fable of which Aesop would have been proud.

"I made a dumb mistake, Trooper Burnett. I did something you should never do. I went down to Mill Creek by myself to take another look at the crime scene where that bow hunter accidentally killed Officer Cornwell. While there, I heard movement up at our first crime scene. So, I walked up to have a look. On my way there, I stumbled and fell on my pocket knife, the one I had just cut a cane pole with. I's going do a little fishing while I was down there, you see?"

He filed no official report on the incident, but he personally visited Foster Realty. In a mad-as-hell rage, he told Bruce Foster, "You get a cover over that collapsed mine shaft! Get it recorded on your deed at the court house as an unsafe ground opening. Put some warning signs around it, too, for God's sake. A good hunting dog could fall into that hole. Don't be stingy about it, neither. Cover it the right way. Hear what I'm telling you, Bruce?"

Homer's gold tooth, skull, and other decayed teeth are still stored at the Fannin County Sheriff's Office. School children on field trips find it awesome. According to Sheriff Darby, no one ever came looking for Homer. It was to be expected though. Homer was a drifter and had few mountain relatives who ever knew his whereabouts. As a troublesome young man, he shook the dirt off his feet and left for Florida. His closest next of kin assumed he'd gone back and was buried there.

Lee Ellen's son, stationed in Iraq, could not come home for her funeral due to the ongoing war. After his tour of duty, for a month, each day he visited his mom's grave site at Farnswell Baptist Church. On his birthday, he visits and places pink roses on her grave. Today, he is a law enforcement officer for the Atlanta Police Department. He never saw his mom's dream cabin site, where today fern and moss and honeysuckle vines thrive.

Jeff, now retired, and Ole Blue, occasionally stop by the site when hunting. He's still off the grid. He fishes, grows a garden, and chops firewood. Together, they do a lot of porch sitting. They watch Mill Creek's never ending flow and he ponders—why people can't forgive, why some are violent, and why a God of mercy allows evil things to happen. When lonely, he often thinks about what life would have been like, if twice he had not lost Lee.

Only Ole Blue and Sheriff Darby know the full truth regarding Lee's death. The remaining lies, misconceptions and the locket are buried at the bottom of that collapsed mine shaft, down on Mill Creek.

Things in the North Georgia Mountains are never what they seem. Mountain people have a unique culture. That does not mean they are at odds with the morals, myths, and beliefs in justice of non-mountain folks. They simply have a different understanding of the phrase Blind Justice—the lies we bury serve and protect all.

———————

Acknowledgement

Many people helped make this book what it is. Two groups went beyond the call of duty. They are my fellow Writers Society members. The groups are respectively led by Lawrence Wertan of The Toccoa Literary and Chicken Pot Pie Society and Mary Ann Wright of the Clarkesville Writers Society. I am deeply indebted to each group for their labor of love.

Others encouraged me to "keep on writing" when I felt doing otherwise was more prudent. To them, The Poetry Company Readers, I offer my heartfelt gratitude. You kept me keeping on.

Lastly, one particular person's words continue to inspire and direct me. Gordon Sawyer influenced thousands in my small corner of the world. His words regarding my talent as a writer remain with me. After reading my first book, *Memoir's of a Chicken Catcher*, he told me, "Don't stop writing. People will enjoy reading your book long after you and I are gone." Thank you Gordon. May your legacy of contributing to the history and literature of the South live on.

ABOUT THE AUTHOR

JOE COBB CRAWFORD is a licensed professional electrical engineer with a passion for story telling. He has a Master of Science degree in engineering from The University of Tennessee. A native of Southern Appalachia, he honed his writing skills by attending the Iowa Summer Writing Festival and two writers groups located in Clarkesville and Toccoa, Georgia. The Blue Ridge Mountains are the setting and material source for all five of his books and include: *The Poetry Company: Memoirs of a Chicken Catcher, When The Chickens Come Home To Roost, Mountain Shadow Memories, Have Books, Will Travel, and What The Bookman Saw.* He resides on Lake Hartwell in northeast Georgia, with his wife of forty-eight years, Susan, a retired teacher and principal.

Other Books by Joe Crawford:

**The Poetry Company:
Memoirs of a Chicken Catcher**

When The Chickens Come Home To Roost

Mountain Shadow Memories

What the Bookman Saw

Available where fine southern books are sold

www.thelieswebury.com
